touching winter

a novel in four parts

touching winter

a novel in four parts

by

Ron Rozelle

TCU Press
Fort Worth, Texas

Library of Congress Cataloging-in-Publication Data

Rozelle, Ron, 1952-
Touching winter : a novel in four parts / by Ron Rozelle.-- 1st.
p. cm.
ISBN 0-87565-308-1 (alk. paper)
I. Title.
PS3568.O994T68 2005
813'.54--dc22
2005002969

Printed in Canada

Book design and
Linocut illustrations by
Barbara Mathews Whitehead

for Karen

tēi kallistēi

How senseless to dread whatever lies before us
when, night and day, the boats,
strong as horses in the wind,
come and go,

bringing in the tiny infants
and carrying away the bodies of the dead.

Billy Collins
"November"

He's been alone for four days now.

Four mornings and afternoons and three nights since he watched the little car make its way down his hill, out his gate, on to the farm-to-market road toward town, then disappear behind a stand of trees that has swallowed other cars. He watched the exact place where the car vanished for a long few minutes before going in and washing the breakfast dishes and putting them away.

Now it is supper time of the fourth day.

He ponders options. Not meaningful ones of any great consequence, just tiny ones concerning food. A fried egg sandwich, maybe. Or a bowl of cereal. A can of chili. A baked potato would be good, but that's out. He has long had an aversion to potatoes being cooked in microwaves, maintaining that the only good baked potato is actually baked, *slowly, in a lather of garlic butter and cracked peppercorns inside a second skin of aluminum foil. And he doesn't intend to wait for the better part of an hour for his supper. So a can of soup, perhaps. Crackers. A beer.*

He rummages through the odds and ends drawer in his kitchen and locates the can opener that he bought in town for two bucks that replaced an electric one and two clever, expensive hand-held models that didn't work. He turns the opener in his hand and tries to read where it was made, and by whom. But the letters are too small and he's left his reading glasses somewhere in another room. He's almost seventy-two years old and he hasn't been able to read fine print for years without his glasses. He learned that long ago. Other things—like two dollar can openers often being more dependable than costly, fancier ones—he has only recently begun to figure out.

That, and the fact that the little car won't be coming back up his hill.

This afternoon, out on his front porch, he looked up past the scarred place where the fire had been to the topmost branch of the tallest tree on his ridge, where a handsome red-tailed hawk often looked back at him. Then a car of about the same size and color as the car he was looking for slowed down on the road, and his heart made a little thump that was altogether different from the fuss it has been making for some time now. Then the car went on, slow enough for him to see that it was a different color after all. A different make.

The hawk wasn't there either.

When the telephone rings he reaches quickly for it and his heart executes another tiny gyration. But it is only his friend from town.

"Your visitor gone?" Eugene wants to know.

"Gone. Left the morning after the fire."

Quiet, now. He can hear the small thing in his chest making its usual muted racket. Sending its hollow, wispy message, like the rustling of dry leaves. Soon, it says. Not much longer now.

"You haven't been to dinner lately," Eugene says. All those years in Houston it had been lunch; here it is dinner.

"Tomorrow's Monday," Eugene tells him. "Billie might make meat loaf."

He rubs his chest a little. Pushes the nagger away for the moment.

"She might make liver, too," he says. "There's no way of

knowing what Billie's going to cook."

He conjures up the image of Eugene standing in his own kitchen in town, talking on the telephone. Eugene was an ugly child, his ears bigger than they ought to have been. The town boys called him Jug Ears and Bing Crosby, but it hadn't seemed to bother him. Later, in high school, he and Eugene threw a couple of ineffective punches at each other behind the gymnasium one afternoon over the affections of a girl named Della who had gone on to die of tuberculosis a few years later. Now Eugene is an old man, like him. He glimpses a barefoot boy of seven or eight standing in the dirt road beside the old post office that was later replaced by the one that was itself later replaced. Then he is just as briefly the high schooler rubbing his unattractive jaw, hoping, at least, for a drop or two of blood for the benefit of the doomed Della. Now he is the old man standing by the wall phone in his kitchen, his trousers hitched up too high, his ears still too big.

"She's never made liver," Eugene says. "That I can recall."

When the conversation is over, when he has promised that he will come to dinner soon—which he knows is a lie that will be forgiven—he looks out the window over the sink to see if there are any visitors. He marvels, more and more, at what a good memory is capable of. At how a person can stand in his own house and look out a window and somebody that's been dead and gone for a full half century or more might smile and wave at him from the yard.

Nobody today. Just the fading light of a November afternoon filtering down through the trees, falling in splotches on the dark grass. The edge of the shed that he can see still looks odd in its fresh coat of paint. When he came back the shed had needed more attention than the house. More boards replaced. More shoring up. As if, being smaller, it hadn't fared as well against summer sun and winter cold, and rain, and hard autumn winds that picked away at everything. And against the worst thing: all that time. Decades of it.

He reaches into the cabinet and makes his decision. Soup. Bean with Bacon. Hearty fare, he figures, in anticipation of the first strong cold front that is due sometime tomorrow. The first good norther of the season heralded by the Weather Channel and a couple of long strings of geese that he watched from the porch.

The first and the last, he realizes.

He smiles at that as he opens the can with his two dollar opener. He nods at the rightness of it. Much of his time lately has been spent thinking of things being made right.

And how he wishes he had been better at it.

one

the boy who touched winter

i

Here was a nest that needed dealing with. Red wasps as wide as nickels clung to it; others swarmed all over it, darting in low under the awning of the shed and into the open windows and then out again over the yard and what was left of the garden and into East Texas in general. Though they had the disposition and aggressiveness of cornered cats, none of this bunch had popped anybody yet that the boy knew of. But it was only a matter of time, so he'd tell his grandfather about it.

Then the old man would roll up a section of the *Tyler Morning Telegraph*—today's, if he had already read it—into a bouquet-looking business, one end bunched up in his big fist and the other spread out open. Then he'd set a match to the wide end and, when it was burning to his satisfaction, he'd just walk up under the grape-like cluster of wasps and hold it over it like he might put a cover over a pound cake. The entire matter would have to be conducted quick enough to destroy the nest without so much as singeing the paint on the shed and, when he was done, he would toss the torch down and stomp it until little flimsy blisters of black paper floated around. He'd use the part of the newspaper that hadn't burned to slap the nest down. The wasps that had been unfortunate enough to be on it would fall away like dried husks; their surviving brethren would swarm around for a minute or two and then go on off and make a new plan.

The boy's mother had fussed often about the old man's method of extermination, saying that he would burn the whole place down around them one of these days, and then what would they do? But he hadn't yet. The boy watched the procedure every time it was conducted, and knew that he could do it equally as well, provided he had something to stand on. He also knew that the chances of him being allowed to get that close to the house or the shed with a burning newspaper were roughly equivalent to him being told to drive the pickup into town to get a couple of sacks of horse and mule feed. He was ten.

He was neither tall nor short, according to the classifications employed by the society of children he attended school with. Nor had he ever been specifically identified as handsome or ugly, intelligent or stupid, graceful or awkward, blessed or cursed. He fell contentedly into a middle ground.

He counted the red wasps on the nest so that he could give his grandfather an accurate report. The dog beside him, called Fred, watched him do it. His original name had been Fritz, mutually agreed upon by both man and boy and inspired by the *Katzenjammer Kids,* which they read together in the funny papers. But his mother had vetoed Fritz, holding that it was much too German for a dog that belonged to a boy whose father was off fighting in the war. The grandfather had said that, since his son was in the South Pacific, it was unlikely that he was fighting anybody named Fritz. But she hadn't given in—she never did—but had approved calling the dog Fred, which was the closest translation of Fritz that the boy could come up with and was sufficiently American to satisfy her.

The grandfather had driven over to a neighboring farm back in the spring, saying that he was going there to discuss a section of fence that needed new posts in some places and new barbed wire in others. And he had returned with this pup, just two days off the teat, and so small that he was almost lost in his huge hands. The boy had reached up and nuzzled the small face and offered a finger that was taken.

"I guess I'll call him Fritz," he had said. "Not Hans."

"That's right," the old man had said, as if he had already made up his own mind about it.

He had been Fritz for most of the rest of that afternoon, and Fred ever since. The boy would never have given his mother the satisfaction of knowing it, but he believed Fred to be a more appropriate name anyway, since the dog didn't look to be a German breed. In fact, he didn't appear to be of *any* determined breed, but more of a Heinz 57 variety. Fred was, he reasoned, as common as he was himself.

"Fourteen," he said, not sure if some of the wasps were under the ones that he could see. "And more flying around." Fred wagged his tail in agreement.

The hills off in the distance were blue in the late afternoon, the elms and oaks and pecans up closer already more red and yellow than green. Three insulted mockingbirds chased a hawk in the direction of the field that he and his grandfather called the big pasture and his mother referred to, more romantically, as the high meadow. His mother read a good many novels.

The grandfather had been off in the truck when he had gotten home from school, either tending to the cattle or the land, the two things he most often tended to. Now the truck rattled up the dirt road and came to a stop under the big cottonwood tree at the edge of the yard. By the time the old man had unfolded his tall, lanky frame out of the cab, the boy and the dog were beside him.

The wide hand that made a slow swipe at the boy's hair was as sun-baked and wrinkled as his face.

"Did you manage to learn anything today?" he asked, as Fred pawed at his khaki trousers and his boots.

The boy nodded, though he couldn't recall that he had.

"Get in any trouble?" Then he winked, the leathery place beside his eye squinting into yet another crease.

"No, sir."

The grandfather touched the boy's shoulder a couple of times as they walked toward the porch.

"Well, that's fine," he said. His jaw was bulged out with an impressive wad of chewing tobacco that he would have to tilt out into his hand and toss away before they went in.

"There's a big nest with fourteen red wasps on it on the back of the shed," the boy told him, tumbling the words out that he had been perfecting for a good half hour. "And lots more buzzing around, like the Japs at Pearl Harbor."

The grandfather listened with the attention that he would give to a banker or a veterinarian or a friend.

"Well, we'll have to get 'em," he said. Then he stopped walking, and cocked one ear up just a bit.

"Listen," he said, and held a finger the texture of a narrow, much-used rope aloft to keep him quiet.

"Honkers," he said after a moment, then he turned and looked off into the cloudless November sky.

They came in over the big pasture, high up and almost out of sight. Sixty or so, the end of the longer leg of the V wandering slowly left and right, like a string blowing in a slight breeze.

"That big norther's chasin' them," the grandfather said. He reached up and pinched the crest of his hat and removed it, either to get a better view or in homage to the geese. The boy didn't know which. The old man's hair was cut short by the barber in town every week, leaving barely enough of the coarse gray thatch to comb. The indention of the hat's band crossed his forehead like a line drawn with a ruler.

The boy nodded, and watched the geese slide across the perfectly still afternoon.

"We already knew that," he said. "We heard it on the radio last night."

The grandfather watched the birds for a moment longer, then put his hat back on, and looked at the boy.

"That's right," he said, as he went on toward the porch. "And now we've got it from a more dependable source."

At supper, the boy watched the grandfather as he leaned down over his plate. He scraped the pot liquor from purple-hulled peas along with a wedge of cornbread and took an occasional sip of coffee from the cup that he lifted up like he would pick an apple or a pear from a tree. The boy couldn't remember ever seeing the old man use the handle of a cup, as if he considered the delicate little curl of porcelain either too fancy to fool with or too small to be manageable with his big hand. He drank coffee with all three of his meals, and sometimes made another pot at night, if he stayed up later than he usually did, working on his accounts book or listening to the programs and the war news on the radio with the boy. He took sugar in his coffee, three spoonfuls stirred slowly in, which didn't seem to affect his weight any more than the caffeine affected his sleep; he appeared never to gain nor lose weight, and he slept like the dead. These things were balanced out, the boy figured, by the fact that his grandfather rarely ate anything sweet—other than an infrequent few bites of pie or cobbler to be gracious to the person who made it—and never slept in the daytime.

His son—the boy's father—was even bigger than the old man. He was wider in the shoulders and thicker throughout with a massive neck that seemed to grow out of his shirt like a post oak. And he had the same big hands, like his father's, that could grasp a fence post and lift it, and could jerk a mule along that had a different idea.

The boy's mother, picking at her own food now, was tiny in comparison. His parents made an odd looking couple, like some barnyard animal and a bird. An unlikely pair.

"We'll need some more wood for the fireplace," she said. She rolled a piece of pork around with her fork. "If we're in for a cool snap."

The grandfather looked at the boy.

"We'll bring it up in the morning from the pile, won't we?"

The next day was a Saturday.

"We shouldn't need much," she said. There was barely enough food on her plate to cover up the blue cornflower design. "The weather's been so nice, I doubt it'll get very cold."

"It'll get cold enough," the grandfather said, reaching over to lift out another slab of cornbread; golden crumbs fell away from it into the skillet. "This here will be a blue norther, I'm thinking."

She prodded the piece of pork once more, then sank her fork gently into it, as if she might actually eat it eventually.

"The man on the radio didn't say anything about it getting that cold," she said.

He chewed the bread slowly, then took a sip from the coffee.

"I didn't hear it from the man on the radio," he said.

The very last light of the afternoon came in pale and sad at the windows. It was spread out over the cabinets of the kitchen and the floral print wallpaper like a faint wash. It fell on the stove and the ice box and the table where they ate all their meals, though there was a fancier table at the end of the parlor that had belonged to the boy's mother's mother, whom he had never known. The light fell on the slender, gangly frame of the grandfather, who sat awkward and hunched in his chair, and on the boy's mother, small and straight-backed in hers, and on the boy. The light slid across the feed store calendar on the wall, slicing it into half-shadow and half-light, like it was doing outside, the boy knew. The bunch of trees between their place and the big pasture and the longer bunch down by the creek would be dark now, nothing more than a black smudge to anybody standing on the front porch. But the fields and the tops of hills would still be blanketed with a soft, wispy light that only came at the very tail-end of cloudless days. When white-tailed deer stepped nervously out of the woods into the edges of pastures to feed; when red-tailed hawks swooped low in search of field mice or baby rabbits that would be the last chance of a meal before darkness enveloped everything.

"What's a *blue* norther?" the boy wanted to know.

"It's a big one," the old man said. "An awful cold and blustery one."

Fred barked outside, probably at a squirrel, or a dove cooing. Or a raccoon or two out early, poking around to see what the garbage can had to offer. Fred had never been in the house; as a small pup he had slept—or howled, more often—in a tall-sided crate in the shed. The boy's mother wouldn't abide animals in the house.

"Why's it called blue?"

The grandfather leaned forward, resting his elbows on the table, cradling his cup in both hands.

"It's so cold it's blue," he said. He lowered the cup to the table, and pushed the plate away a few inches. "I can remember some that were so cold they were icy blue, almost black. They filled up the whole sky comin' in, with thunder and lightning that put any July Fourth fireworks to shame. And *cold?*" He clicked his tongue against his teeth and squinted one eye shut. "All of a sudden like. A fella could be standing there in his shirtsleeves with sweat on his neck, and in no time at all he'd be wishing for a jacket, and headed for a heater."

The boy thought about that. Then he raked his cornbread through what was left on his plate, exactly as the old man had done.

"When is this thing supposed to get here?" he asked.

"Tomorrow," the grandfather said. "Sometime tomorrow. By tomorrow night we'll have to have us a good fire roaring in there on the grate."

"You've been talking about it for two days, and it's been on the radio and in the newspaper. And there was those geese," the boy said. He pushed the cornbread tight against the plate, leaving a clean, shiny place filled with the tiny blue flowers, framed by food. In the morning, for his breakfast, his mother would slice through a piece of the left-over cornbread, toast it with butter, and spread it over with some of the preserves that she kept in abundant supply, owing to an over-productive tree in the yard that the old man called fig proud.

"If it's comin,' why don't it come on?"

The old man leaned back in his chair and stretched a little. He swirled his coffee around in the cup, and held it out away from him.

"It's had a long way to travel," he finally said. "From way up at the top of the world, I expect. And down across all those big ice fields—whole fields of just ice, like we have in taters and beans. And all of Canada—which ain't no little place, itself—and then down through Montana and Wyoming and over some mighty tall mountains and then through some of Colorado and Kansas and Oklahoma before it even *gets* to Texas. Then it'll still be a ways off from our place."

He took a sip from his coffee, and sat quiet. He had expended an uncommonly large cluster of words at one time, the boy knew. The old man waited a moment, like he would wait for a bucket to fill back up at a faucet.

"Why," he finally said, leaning toward the boy, "I'll bet when that big rascal gets here, we'll be able to smell those fir forests from Canada and Wyoming, and maybe the corn fields in Kansas." He winked then.

The boy knew the minty fragrance of fir, but had to think a minute before he could recall the sweet smell of ripe corn in a field, and the musty smell of the dried variety that he threw out in handfuls to the chickens.

"You oughtn't to tell him that sort of thing," the boy's mother said. "It's not the truth."

The grandfather gave that some thought, rubbed the back of his neck, and produced the little down-turned smile that the boy had never seen on any other creature, human or animal. He had looked for it there, and had so far only found it in the old man.

"It's the truth that it's coming," his grandfather said. "And it's coming through all of those places. And it's the truth that when I walk by this kitchen window on a day that you've been baking bread and the breeze blows through here, that I can smell it. The same as I don't ever have any difficulty knowing where I am when I walk by the cattle pens." He stopped there and drank some of his coffee. "So why ain't it the truth that a strong north wind can bring along a little taste of where it's been?"

She gave enough of a snort to discount the whole notion, but the boy finished his supper with ears of corn and boughs of fir needles swirling around in his thoughts.

His mother smiled just a little, then stopped herself, as if she had suddenly discovered what she was doing.

"I sure never heard of such a thing," she said, putting her silverware in her plate. Done.

Later, after the boy had listened to *Fibber Magee and Molly*—more of it given over to the selling of Lucky Strike cigarettes and war bonds than he would have liked, and not enough of Gildersleeve—he heard the other two, still in the kitchen. They were talking low enough to believe they couldn't be heard. Which they couldn't have, if he hadn't cracked his bedroom door and stood beside it.

The grandfather had listened to the radio with him, then had gone in the kitchen to boil a half a pot of coffee. The boy's mother had read for a while on the sofa—*Rebecca,* from the little library in town—but had smiled a few times at the program, and had even laughed once or twice. Then the boy had been sent off to bed, and she had decided on a glass of milk to help her sleep.

The conversation had started with the grandfather saying that he intended to replace a few rotten boards here and there, and then had moved to the need for new Sunday shoes for the boy, and something or other for the hay rake that the boy couldn't quite make out.

"We might need to get a loan," the boy's mother said. "If we don't have enough hay for all winter, and have to end up buying some."

The boy could hear nothing for long enough to convince both him and his mother that there wouldn't be any response.

"I know how you feel about it," she said.

"We won't be buying any hay," the old man said. "We'll feed out less, and if we start to run low, we can borrow some 'til spring. From one of the other fellas."

The boy could hear the slight clatter of her putting away the dishes that had been drying beside the sink. Maybe one of the clinks was his grandfather's coffee cup being lowered back into its saucer.

"But what if nobody else has any, either. Then where will we be?"

It was quiet, again. Until the old man's voice came low and sure of itself through the parlor and the small hallway and to the boy.

"We'll be where we've been before." The old man's voice floated through the house like Fred Allen's and Jack Benny's did when the radio was turned on. "And where we'll likely be again."

The boy could hear the clock in the parlor ticking. It was a not very large or particularly handsome clock that his mother had inherited from her family; it sat on the exact center of the mantle, on a white doily. Each tick reverberated through the wood of its case, down the mantle, into the skeleton of the little house, along the planks of the floor, and into the doorframe that the boy leaned against.

"If Robert was here," his mother said, not very loud, or with very much confidence, "we could have planted and made more hay."

Quiet, again. And then her small voice one more time.

"And more truck crops."

The parlor clock continued to send out its precise little jolts. The boy pressed the side of his face against the doorframe, trying to feel them.

"But he's not here," the grandfather said. He wasn't much given to ifs.

"No," she said.

"And he could be," she added. "And that's . . ." There were no more dishes clinking against each other now. She would be draping her dishtowel over the side of the sink. "That's the thing, you see." It wasn't a question, certainly not one that the grandfather would have answered.

"He didn't have to go," she said, for the first time using the words that both the old man and the boy knew she had been thinking. Using the words that had been simmering in her since August.

"They're not drafting married men," she went on. "Not yet. And even if they do, he'd have been able to . . ."

There was enough of a silence now for the boy to figure that she had sat down across the table from the grandfather. The milk in her glass would be frothy and rich, separated just that morning in the machine that his grandfather kept tightened and maintained as if it were the single mechanism that kept the whole place going.

"To what?" the old man asked her.

"You know what. Teddy Vernor didn't have to go, and he hasn't got a family. Nor even a wife."

"Teddy Vernor's uncle is head of the draft board," the grandfather said.

"I know he is," she said. An edge of resentment had worked its way into her voice. "And I know what he thinks of Robert. And the other men on that board, too. They like him. And they'd take him off the list if he asked them to."

The boy listened closer now, straining to hear whatever might come. An owl sang out up toward the big pasture. A smaller one—or farther off—answered him.

"And what sort of a man would that make Robert?" the grandfather said.

She talked louder now. Sharper.

"The sort that's *here.* With his family. On this place. The sort that can take a little extra advantage of a situation every once in a while. Like other people."

The boy knew that it was completely still in the kitchen now, that darkness filled up the curtainless windows, and that his mother would be sitting stoic and sad and tired, all at the same time. He knew that the little down-turned smile would have worked its way into his grandfather's hard face.

"Other people," the grandfather said. The two words were like expelling bad air, almost too low for the boy to even hear them.

The boy took the world atlas, as wide as a chair seat, to bed with him and found all the places his grandfather had said that the norther would pass. Here was Canada, sprawled out across two of the big pages like one of his mother's quilts draped over the fence on a sunny day. Then he found maps of specific states. Colorado and Kansas. Montana. Wyoming. But he couldn't remember how they all lined up with each other, so he fanned the thick pages back and forth until he found what he wanted: a map of all of North America. Then he could see it clear.

He leaned back into his pillow, propped the atlas against his knees, and moved the tip of his finger slowly down the page, trying to imagine what the geese ahead of the norther would see from so far up. Wide ice fields first, he guessed. White as far as the geese could see in any direction for a long time, days maybe. He didn't know how long. The color under his finger changed then from white to green. So there would be thick forests now that the big birds would be looking down into. And farms and rivers and houses that probably looked tiny from such a height. And lakes. He let the goose that he was occupying slide down low over lakes, so low that he could see fish just under the blue surface. He made them bass like there would be in Texas lakes, but realized that there were probably other kinds of fish up north. He knew well enough that a goose wouldn't be able to see any catfish since catfish lived at the bottoms of lakes and rivers, but he let a few of the fish be catfish anyway. Just for a little variety.

He flew over towns and highways and country roads like the one that went by the farm. And silos and water towers and church steeples. He tried hard to feel what the geese would feel, the hard force that pushed them. The raw, frigid air that filled up the whole sky behind them. The bristly sting of wind stabbing through their feathers. He listened to them singing out to each other in their flight, the high-pitched honks sharp and clear. The lettering on the brown, white-tipped points under his finger said Rocky Mts., and he knew the geese would have to lift up higher here, and sail over them. He looked down now with his goose eyes and saw the steep, snow-covered mountaintops washed in sunlight. He found his own shadow, and those of the other birds. Tiny, dark specks slowly rising and falling across the white crags and valleys.

After the mountains, it was nighttime. A clear, cloudless night full of stars that would be hidden soon by the norther. The boy knew that geese flew at night—unlike hawks, who never did—because he had heard them up there. He had seen the slight movement of their wings reflected in pale moonlight. The world below him was almost all dark now, with only the feeble glow of little towns twinkling hazy and inferior and unimportant under all that dark and those countless pinpoints of perfect light.

His finger hesitated over the letters that spelled Dallas, because he was torn between wanting to see it in daylight or darkness. The tall buildings and busy streets must be awfully impressive from such a height, but all the lights that such a city would produce might be even more so. He yawned, and wasn't quite sure how the city slipped by beneath him.

By the time he had flown over Tyler and then the fields and woods just before his own town, the atlas had fallen away, and he was sound asleep before he even got to the house he was sleeping in.

In the morning, after they had brought up the wood to the porch, and after they had burned the wasp nest and gathered the eggs—in addition to hens, the boy's mother kept two white ducks, of the commonest and meanest variety, because she maintained that ducks' eggs made superior batters—the boy and the grandfather replaced a few rotten boards on the white fence that surrounded the house and the yard. The old man had waited until Saturday to do it, so the boy could be in on it.

The boy had held the boards while the old man sawed them, then held them again for the hammering. Now the grandfather was watching him as he spread oily paint on with a brush that was almost too broad and bulky for him to handle.

"Why don't we paint the whole fence?" the boy wanted to know. "It needs it. And the house."

"People in hell need ice water, too," the old man said. He was the only person known to the boy who could use such a sentence and not sound like he was cursing. If *he* had said it, the old man would have fussed at him. If his mother had been close enough to hear it, she would have sent him out to cut the very switch that she would then employ to slap three or four times across the back of his bluejeans. His grandfather had never whipped him, nor threatened to, his father had just the one time, with a belt, and his mother several more times than that, but never with sufficient force to cause him to even squint.

The grandfather used "hell" and "damn" fairly regularly, "shit" only once that the boy could recall, when he had pounded his thumb with a ballpeen hammer while he was attempting some repair on the hay rake, and nothing more serious or vulgar than that. He had never heard the old man say "goddamn" or "Jesus" like other men sometimes did. And he knew that it wasn't owing to any religious conviction or piety on his grandfather's part; he went to the Baptist church with the family only at Christmas and Easter, and to Wednesday night prayer meetings every great once in a while because he was fond of the singing. He wouldn't have used that sort of language because he knew that it was offensive to some people. Most folks, even pillars of the church, could stand an occasional "hell" and "damn," and didn't seem to mind when Adolph Hitler—or maybe even President Roosevelt, depending on their mood and their bank account—was called a bastard or a son of a bitch. But they drew the line at sacrilege.

"Paint's costly," the grandfather said. He pointed to a place that the boy had missed. "And it's fixin' to be rationed. I imagine they use heaps of paint in the army and the navy." The boy had heard him and his mother talking about the things that would be rationed. The only item that made the old man moan a little, and rub his wide hand across his jaw, was coffee. He'd be hard pressed to make it through even one day without his coffee.

"So we've got to make do with what paint's left in this can here, and then be done with painting for a spell."

The boy used both hands to wield the brush; he slapped it into the place where the board met the fence post.

Thin cattle, their ribs as pronounced under brown hide as the bowed frames of covered wagons in pictures in the boy's reading book at school, sauntered slowly along on the other side of the fence. The cattle moved from one pasture to another several times each day, in search of grass that they had long since eaten down to nothing. Fred barked at the cows, and the boy and the grandfather both told him to hush at the same time and he did. They had broken him of chasing the cattle, but sometimes other dogs came on the place and bothered them. The grandfather had had to have a hard talk with a man up the road about his dogs, since they had caused a cow to back up over its newborn calf and crush it. He had said that he wouldn't like shooting the dogs, but that he would if he had to.

The grandfather counted the cattle. Then he counted them again.

"We're one short," he said. "If she don't come up, we'll have to go look for her here directly."

The boy paid attention to his painting. He swatted at a gnat that had flown up out of the dew-wet grass.

"Maybe it got out of the fence," he said.

The old man shook his head.

"Naw. It's an old one." He looked out at the field the cows had come from. "She's either lagging behind, or she's dead."

"Why would it be dead?" the boy asked. He slapped at the gnat again and nearly dropped the brush. The grandfather took it from him and dabbed slowly at the board.

"I said, it was old. Maybe its time was just up. Like when we found that hawk dead on the ground that time. It hadn't been shot. Another bird hadn't killed it, because another bird wouldn't know how to go about killing a hawk. So it just got old and used up its time. That's all."

He looked at the board they had painted, then moved to another one.

"There's not anything bad about dying, " the grandfather said, as determinedly as if the boy had maintained that there was. "It's as right as being born."

He looked off to the north, over the big pasture and into a clear morning sky. "That blue norther you're so anxious to get here is bringing death right along with it." He pointed the paint brush up at the massive cottonwood that loomed over them. "It'll blow most of these leaves on out, then the cold weather that'll settle in behind it will kill everything that's left in the garden, and most everything in your mother's flower bed." He pointed toward the house. "Honeysuckle and wisteria'll shrivel up and dry out, and finally the trees will be nekkid as jaybirds. The plants and bushes'll be dead." He dabbed some paint on the new board. "Winter will come on, and even the land will be dead."

The boy had looked at the things the old man had pointed to, and had listened to what he had said.

"But trees and bushes grow back," he said. "Hawks and cows are just . . . dead."

"Well," the grandfather said, "there'll be a new calf to take the place of that old cow. Ain't that right? And I've never noticed any lack of hawks floating around. Have you?"

The grandfather dipped the brush into the paint, slid the bristles along the rim of the can, then pulled it slowly along the new board.

"Hawks and cows and trees all do the same thing," he said. "Every living thing spends out its time, then it makes way for the next batch. That's the right way of it."

The boy looked at him for a long moment.

"What about people?"

"Ain't people living things?" the old man asked.

The boy didn't answer that, since he wasn't any more likely to answer a stupid question than the grandfather was.

"People, too," the old man said.

He laid the brush on top of the can, lowered himself slowly down to sit on the ground, and leaned back against a fence post. He pinched the apex of his hat, lifted it off, then sat it carefully on the grass beside him.

"The only difference is," he said, "trees and hawks and cows and everything else do it *right*." He pulled his plug of tobacco out of his back pocket and his pocket knife out to the front, sliced off a section of gummy tobacco, lifted it to his mouth on the knife blade, then worked it firmly into the back of his jaw.

"They do what right?" the boy asked.

"Living and dying," the old man answered, delivering such lofty words in the same way that he would say salt and pepper. He prodded the tobacco with his tongue a few times, to get the juices flowing. "It's only people that can get it all crossed up."

"What does that mean? Crossed up?"

"Well, let's just suppose that you don't do what you're supposed to." He closed his knife and slid it back into his pocket. "Let's just say you waste your time. You squander it. You lie to folks, or take advantage of them. Then when people think of you, they think of that lie and how you can't be trusted. And that means that when you die, then all that bad talk and feeling hangs on after you. And that's how people will remember you. As a scoundrel. And a liar."

He leaned forward enough to reach a tuft of grass with his fingers. He swished through it a couple of times, like he always did to the boy's hair. Then he pulled up a few of the sprigs and let them go again.

"Or like when a person doesn't do the right thing. Or when a fella doesn't stand for something, because it's hard." He spat some of the tobacco juice now, a dark heavy glob that sailed perfectly between the planks of the fence. "*Especially* when it's hard. Like your daddy, off over there in this war. That's one of the things people will remember about your daddy one of these days. That's one of the things they'll say about him. That he stood up for something, and he went off to fight in the war."

The sun was higher, the day warmer than average for November.

Something startled a covey of quail between them and the big pasture. The birds burst up into the sunshine, then darted off to the south with the agility and purpose of a single creature. They watched them go.

"But people wouldn't say anything bad about Daddy if he didn't go," the boy said. "He didn't *have* to go." He said it like he had thought it all out for himself and hadn't heard it listening to conversations he wasn't supposed to hear.

The grandfather listened, then nodded.

"Well," he said, after a moment, "I expect he felt like he had to. And then, if he hadn't of done it, he would have said those things to himself. About himself."

He looked out at where the quail had been.

"And that would be worse than other people saying them."

He got more comfortable against the post, and laid one long leg out flat. He rested his forearm on his other knee.

"You see, a hawk nor a tree nor even Fred there," he pointed to the dog, who sat contentedly beside where the boy was standing, "they don't have to fret about any of this. Because they just do what they're supposed to do, and then, when it's their time, they just die."

The boy's mother opened the back door, stepped out on the porch, poured some coffee grounds out into her flower bed, and went back in. She maintained that coffee grounds were good fertilizer, better even than horse manure.

"That's the way a human being ought to behave, too." A little cloud of steam rose up off the flower bed. "To my way of thinking."

Fred went over to the bed and smelled of the grounds, determined them to be not of any use to him, and went back to his same spot beside the boy.

"A human being ought to mind their own business, provide for their family, and get all their feuds settled and their fences mended. And they ought to clean up any mess that they've made, and make things right that they did wrong. And then when it comes time for a fella to die, then all he has to do is just sit down somewhere and do it." He looked at the boy. "You see? Because he's done the best he could and made a good showing. He's done what he set out to do, and done it the best that he could. Then he can go on. Like that cow down there in that pasture—if she's dead—and like all these trees and things that that norther will kill. It'll be as natural and right as that."

The grandfather shook his head just a little, and the downturned smile appeared. He pulled himself up, then dusted his hands off against each other.

"Well, lookey here," he said, running his big hand through the boy's hair. "I've gone and preached a whole damn sermon. And didn't even pass the plate."

The cow wasn't dead. They found her that afternoon down by the creek, in seemingly good health and spirits in the shade of a sycamore tree. The grandfather said that it just hadn't struck her fancy, apparently, to walk all the way over to another pasture just because everybody else was going. And that maybe she had just figured it out that there wasn't any more grass to eat over there than there was over here. So why bother?

The boy spent much of that afternoon in the front porch swing, looking off in the direction that the grandfather had shown him the norther would come from. North was directly over the big pasture, the old man had told him, and that's where the thing would come. All that was there now, over the curved rim of sun-dabbled grass, was a cloudless afternoon sky as blue as a lake.

Thanksgiving was almost two weeks away, and this would be the first cold spell of the year to speak of. There had been some cool mornings, one or two even cool enough for the boy's mother to make him wear his jacket to school. There had even been something close enough to a Jack Frost for the grandfather to light the heaters in the bathroom and the kitchen one chilly dawn. But this norther would be the first blast of the season. And thc grandfather held that it would be a dandy.

The old man passed by the porch from time to time, on his way to or from one chore or another. He stopped once, took out his pocket watch and looked at it, then studied the north sky, which didn't seem to be involved in anything more than providing an area for a few birds to drift through.

"It'll come," he said.

At supper—collard greens and corn relish and the last of the pork roast they had had the night before—the boy's mother said that this one had passed them by apparently, or had stalled out. She had pulled the kitchen door open a few inches, to let some of the heat from the stove out.

"The man on the radio said they sometimes stall out."

The grandfather chewed the stringy pork. He winked at the boy.

"Not this one," he said. "This one's too big for that. It couldn't any more just pull up and stop than a rock could stop sinking to the bottom of a lake."

"It slipped by us then," the mother said.

The boy had spent all of the day wanting it to come. Watching for it. Once, on the front porch, he had made sure that neither of the others was around, then he had leaned forward and sniffed at the air. Because maybe, he figured, it sent a little of the smell of what it was carrying out in front of it, like it pushed along geese. But the air of the porch had been as empty as the sky. And, by supper, he had reached the same conclusion that his mother had.

"It might have," the old man said. He took up his coffee cup in both big hands, swirled it around a little. "Most of it might have moved by on one side or the other. But we'd have seen it; we'd have seen the clouds from it. And heard it. Nothing that big can *slip* anywhere."

He looked at the last puddle of coffee in the cup.

"It just ain't here yet," he said.

The man came just a few minutes after they had finished their supper. The boy and the grandfather watched first the dust that was thrown up by the man's car and then the car itself. A Ford, moving not all that quickly up the unpaved road, turning, then up to their fence. The grandfather lifted himself slowly up from the porch swing and met the man under the cottonwood.

"Your renter's done lit out," the man said, slapping his fedora against his small thigh, as if he had ridden a horse, hard, out to them. He was a short man, a few years younger than the grandfather, in an pair of old suit pants that came almost to his chest. He wore suspenders over a white shirt; his necktie was short and wide and particularly colorful—huge splashy blossoms—for such a small, drab individual. He owned one of the two grocery stores in the town.

"He run up a little bill with me, which I ought to have had better sense than to have allowed, and he promised to come in and take care of it today. But, hell . . ." He nodded at the boy's mother, who was standing on the porch. "He didn't."

He pointed now in the general direction of the small, dilapidated house and the four acres around it, several miles away. The grandfather had lived there until his wife died, and now he kept it rented out when he could.

"So I drove out there after I closed up the store. And it's empty as can be. Front door was wide open. They even took the dishpan, which I expect belongs to you."

The grandfather shook his head slowly. The boy wondered if it meant that the pan hadn't been his, or if he was just responding to this new situation.

"He seemed like a good enough fella," the grandfather said.

"Hell," the grocer said. "They're wetbacks." He frowned. "We both of us ought to have had better sense."

Everybody was quiet for a moment. The grocer took out a crumpled pack of cigarettes and dug one out.

"Won't do any good to tell the sheriff." He spat out the last word in a single syllable, emitting a sound like a closing door might make. "He'd likely just laugh at our stupidity." He almost smiled then, with the cigarette dangling from the corner of his mouth. "Won't do any good to set out after them. They had them a vehicle—a Chevrolet I think—and they're long gone by now. Probably back down to Mexico."

He struck a match and held it to the bent cigarette, shook the flame out and tossed the match away, then looked for a long moment into the south. As if he might actually locate the little family there.

"I guess we learned ourselves a lesson," he said. Then he blew a long line of smoke out into the fading light of the late afternoon.

The grandfather thanked him for driving out to tell him.

"They owed for the last two months," was what the boy's mother had to say, when the man had gone.

The grandfather sat down heavily on the porch swing. He took off his hat and set it down beside him.

"I told you to go get that money," the boy's mother said. She was still standing by the door, still holding her dishtowel. "I *told* you how those people behave. And how we'd end up regretting letting them move in there at all."

The old man sat still in the swing. The boy sat on the step with Fred.

"They had those children," the grandfather said, after a moment. "And then their baby got sick."

The boy watched the dust behind the grocer's Ford until it disappeared behind some trees.

"They had to pay the doctor and the drug store," the grandfather said. "On account of the baby."

The final light of that afternoon lay on the big pasture and on the open places between the trees. The boy didn't watch it today, like he usually did. He didn't hear the muffled, low rumbling from the north. He watched the old man.

"We were counting on that money," the boy's mother said. She stared at the grandfather for a minute or two, then went back in. The screen door slapped against its frame. A single fly buzzed near the boy, then by the dog, then out over the yard and toward the cottonwood tree. The grandfather continued to sit, perfectly still and straight, on the swing. His big hat sat beside him, like a particularly patient and well-behaved dog.

"I figured him for a better man than that."

He almost whispered it. Not to the boy, or even to himself. He might as well have been saying it to Fred. Or to that fly, which was sweeping low over the yard in the direction of the distant, uneven line where the big pasture met the northern horizon. Where a dark, purple blackness climbed slowly up into the dusk.

The grandfather and the boy would not later be able to agree, or correctly remember, if they had first seen the clouds or heard the thunder.

The norther was darker at the horizon than higher up, so dark that the boy couldn't imagine a deeper, darker color. At school, he sometimes drew pictures of pastures and skies and colored them with crayons, and he didn't think he would be able to press down hard enough with a blue crayon to make a color this dark.

Lightning ignited inside the darkness, popping like flashbulbs under water; several times narrow veins of light ran up and down the sky. Then one strong bolt arced quickly across everything, fragmenting finally into a pitchfork of electric fingers. Thunder rumbled inside the norther. Like explosions deep in caves. Like the angry, muffled grumbling of approaching giants.

The grandfather and the boy watched it for a few minutes from the porch, then walked out into the yard.

The first of the wind was nothing more than a stirring in the topmost branches of trees and in what was left of the grass in the pastures. The boy's mother's azalea bushes moved only slightly at first, then began to dance. Then the wind came stronger. In the mammoth cottonwood, thousands of brown and yellow leaves—each one as large as a saucer—fluttered, like countless venetian blinds flapping open and shut.

Many of the leaves snapped free of their branches and hung motionless for an instant. Then, as a gigantic school of fish might turn and move away from a danger, the innumerable, crinkled parchments floated away from the tree.

The leaves floated over the two of them, slowly at first, as if having to learn the physics of it, then more quickly. The old man and the boy looked up at the ceiling of leaves, and listened to the rustling. The old man said something, but the boy was watching too intently now to pay much attention to it.

Louder thunder cracked inside the norther, then rolled along through it. The wind grew stronger, and pushed the canopy of leaves forward with the determination of frightened birds taking flight.

The first raindrops splattered all around the old man and the boy. The wind was strong in their faces and was full of the smell of rain. Of the absolute promise of it. The chickens in the hen house commenced a unanimous squawking and flapping. Fred barked at them. Or at the wind. Or at life in general.

The first frigid gust came just then. A no-nonsense declaration that things will change now. The boy watched the almost impossibly dark thing over the top of the big pasture, and knew that it was time now for it to be dark anyway, like on any normal day, but that this would be a darkness beyond that daily settling. He felt his grandfather's hand on his shoulder, and he felt the big raindrops splat against his face. And he felt the cold. He raised his hand up and put his palm against it, like he would touch an elephant or an army tank or a dinosaur, if given the opportunity.

The rain came harder then, blown horizontally by the cold wind. And they went in, the old man and the boy to build a fire in the fireplace, and Fred to locate a dry place in the shed.

Later, the fire ate its way through oak and pecan logs, and smoke went up the chimney and out into the blustery, cold night. The fire crackled and the north wind and rain pelted against the windows with a cadence more satisfying than anything that might be on one of their programs, so the old man and the boy sat on the sofa and watched the fire like they usually sat and watched the radio.

The boy's mother had read her book in her usual chair for a while, then had gone to get ready for bed. She had told the boy to get along to his own bed in the next few minutes, then she had hesitated by the door and looked at the two of them in the flickering light of the fire.

"I'm glad for a night like this," she had said. Which had caused them both to look over at her, since she hardly ever made pronouncements in general that didn't involve things that needed doing or things that hadn't been done when they should have been.

"I'm glad for a night to snuggle down deep into the covers," she had told them. Then she had gone down the short hall into her room, to face the winter night emptiness of a double bed that has been long occupied by two people. They heard her door close softly.

They sat quietly for a while.

The boy was ten now, too old to be held in laps, and had, in fact, never been held in laps very often even when he had been smaller and younger. But he scooted over closer to the grandfather on the sofa and, soon, his head was leaning against the hard, bony shoulder. He was close enough to smell the chewing tobacco in the old man's shirt pocket, and even a vestige of the bay rum he splashed on after he shaved. And here was the faint presence of peach brandy, made by some old woman in town and either given or sold to the old man; the boy never knew which. He generally had a sip or two of it after supper—always on the porch and always secure in the knowledge that neither the boy nor his mother knew about it, even though they both did—and on a night like this one he had had more than a couple.

Earlier, the boy had tried hard to smell something in the norther other than rain. He had wanted corn and fir and mountain greenery. And he had even thought he detected something of it once, but now, leaning close against the grandfather, he figured it had just been wishing it to be so. Like he wished that his father was somewhere safe and dry in the South Pacific, farther away even than where this weather had come from. Like he wished that his father was not being threatened by the Japanese, buzzing around like the red wasps on the shed. And that his mother would be happier about things more often, and that there could somehow be more money.

But the boy was ten, fully aware that just wanting something to be one way didn't keep it from actually being another. He leaned closer into his grandfather's side and nestled his head closer against his shoulder. The things he had hoped to smell in the norther might or might not have been there. But here was bay rum and tobacco and peach brandy, as real as the fire crackling and spitting in front of him.

He remembered, then, what the grandfather had said outside, when the huge, delicate assemblage of leaves floated away from the cottonwood tree. He had been too busy, just then, watching it to pay attention to the words. But he heard them now, as clearly as if they were being repeated.

"As long as something like that can happen," the old man had told him, as he had looked up, with the boy, at the accumulation of leaves magically suspended for a moment above them, "then nothing can be too bad."

The boy whispered the words, barely moving his lips. Not making enough of a sound to cause the old man to ask what he had said.

"Nothing can be too bad," the boy whispered.

ii

The annual vigils worked their way into the calendars of the boy and the grandfather as absolutely as birthdays and holidays and the opening of deer season.

Every fall, and sometimes as late as early winter, when the first big promise of arctic air barreled down, heralded by geese and the man on the radio and the *Tyler Morning Telegraph,* they would take up their post in the front yard or, most often, up at the big pasture, which offered more of a front row seat. The process involved several hours of just waiting and paying careful attention to the northern horizon, so they sat, or leaned against a tree or fence posts.

New moons grew from slivers to fullness then back again into nothingness; Christmases and Easters and birthdays drifted by, like logs in a slow moving river. The war ended and the boy's father came home. He marched once down the main street of the little town with other veterans in a parade, then told the boy's mother to pack his uniform away and he never wore it again. Neither did he ever talk about his experiences, other than to mention, on a broiling summer afternoon, that it had been even hotter in the South Pacific. The boy's father didn't, in fact, converse any more often than he had before the war, but fell immediately back into the quiet habit of farming and raising cattle, plodding his way along a seasonal timetable older than the rocks he had to sometimes dig out of newly cleared pasture. Crops were planted and grew and were harvested. Whole generations of cattle were born and were either sold at the livestock auction or produced as many calves as they could generate until, one by one, they finally made one final bleat at the sun or the moon and dropped dead in one of the three pastures that had been their entire worldly experience.

The boy grew taller every year, until the old man sitting beside him waiting for northers was stooped in comparison. Fred the dog sat beside them for eight of the vigils, until one summer when he had a run in with a snake. He had survived numerous bites over the years, but this had been a particularly aggressive copperhead that had kept striking at his neck and his head, and he didn't get up this time. They buried him under the cottonwood tree in the yard.

The boy and the grandfather could never interest the other two members of the family in joining them in the vigils. So they did it by themselves until the boy graduated from high school and went off to find his life's work, which he was sure was not on the farm.

Then came a November when it was just the old man up at the big pasture, leaning against the fence post that he had come to favor because it curved where his back did. It took him longer to walk up there now, and required more of an effort to lower himself down and then stand back up again. He cut himself a generous plug of sweet tobacco and situated it far back in his jaw. Then he leaned back against the fence post and tilted his hat forward just slightly. He had counted six passages of geese in the last couple of days, and the men on the radio and the newspaper had made their predictions, so all he had to do now was wait.

He thought of the boy, of course. And of the dog. He studied his hands for a long moment or two, after he had been there a while, and marveled at how old they had become. He wondered when that had happened. He remembered how his wife, then nothing more than just a girl, had held those hands in her much smaller ones even before the turn of the century. He tried hard to remember exactly what she had looked like then, because lately he had had trouble remembering that. He could recall the old woman that he had looked at in her coffin at the funeral home in town, but he couldn't quite make out the girl that she had been long, long before that.

He must have fallen asleep once, because he snorted loud enough to notice it, then he looked at the sky over the curve of the pasture, and it hadn't changed. He had to stand up and stretch a couple of times, and he walked down to stand under a sycamore tree to make water.

Later, when the first dark edge peeked over the horizon and the first muted rumblings of approaching thunder groaned, he thought of the boy again, because this first glimpse had always been his favorite part. And he thought of his wife—just all of a sudden when he hadn't been intending to—and this time he could see her plainly as a girl again, not an old woman.

The norther, the biggest in several years, climbed up into the evening sky. The last bit of that day's light would have to fight harder than usual to stay, given this new darkness to contend with. The grandfather watched as the light didn't put up any fight at all, but bled into the wispy blue of the approaching storm.

He leaned more comfortably against the fence post and spat a single, heavy glob of tobacco juice as far as he could send it. And if somebody had been there to ask him, he would have been hard pressed to say just what it was that caused him to smile so.

The next morning, the boy hung up the heavy receiver of the only telephone in the Houston boarding house where he shared a room with two other men. He stood there for a long moment and ran his finger up and down the receiver.

"News from home?" the woman who owned the house wanted to know. When the call had come, she had had to pound on his door to wake him up, since he had been out late drinking beer with one of his roommates and hadn't been asleep long.

"Yes, m'am," he said. They had waited until five to call him, knowing that it would wake somebody up who would have to go for him.

He rubbed his jaw, and knew that he would need a shave and a couple of aspirin tablets. Then he'd have to call the foreman at the concrete mixing plant where he worked, who wouldn't be any too happy that he'd be missing a couple of days.

"Breakfast won't be ready for a spell," the woman said. She stood in the hallway in a heavy bathrobe cinched tight at her ample waist. The boy had never seen her in anything other than one of the several floral print dresses that comprised her entire wardrobe. "You going back to bed?"

He shook his head, ran his hand through his hair.

"I'm up now," he said.

When he had bathed, and shaved, and put on clean clothes, he packed his suitcase and walked the nine blocks down to the cement batching plant and saw the foreman, then up to the Greyhound depot. Payday was a few days off, and he had had to borrow the money for a ticket from the third roommate, who didn't waste his money on beer in honky-tonks.

When he had his ticket, he stood outside the bus station and smoked a cigarette. An old man walked by, and he looked, as he always did, for the little down-turned smile. Of course it wasn't there. It wasn't anywhere now. He finished his cigarette and tossed the butt down and tried to sort out what he was feeling. But he wasn't feeling anything. Other than a little hungry and a little hung over. He counted out the money he had left and went inside and bought a Baby Ruth bar and a package of Doublemint gum.

Back outside, he sat on a bench, and waited until time for his bus to leave.

The downtown buildings reflected the morning sun and were golden against the early morning sky. The boy watched the blue as it got darker, as it crept slowly up behind the buildings until the entire northern sky was filled with the darkness. He predicted exactly when he would hear the first thunder and when he would see the muffled explosions of lightning; he'd had considerable experience at it. The American and Texas flags outside the bus station fluttered for a moment or two, then popped and snapped against their ropes. As the first sprinkling of rain splattered against his face, he realized that he was crying.

The wind came harder then; he reached out one hand and felt the rain and the first hint of cold air. He was crying hard enough now for a little girl standing close by to tug at her mother's dress and point to him. He was crying hard enough to have to catch his breath. And that's when the perfectly blended presence of tobacco and bay rum and peach brandy reached him, floating along on the swift air as surely and contentedly as geese winging their way home.

Occasionally a car or a pickup passes by in the darkness at the foot of his hill. The glare from their headlights reaches out into the soft November night just far enough to make dents in the darkness. Families going home after evening services, maybe. Or high school kids out drinking beer and making their way along country roads before another week of school.

None of the lights belong to the little car that he wants to see, of course. He's finally given up on that.

After his soup and crackers he came out here, not interested in the inane offerings on television on such a splendid night. All those years away from here—down in the flat, concrete and steel landscape of Houston—he missed this porch. These hills. These stars. This porch swing, and the larger one that once hung here.

He finds Orion, the hunter, in a sky packed with stars. It is a clear, cool night that often precedes a big norther, as if Nature has done a good cleaning, making sure everything is scrubbed bright before the onslaught of a particularly rambunctious visitor. He listens for geese; hopes for them. For the reassurance of their presence, of things moving along.

None yet. So far there's just been the sound of a car as it passes, and the slight rustling of leaves in the giant cottonwood that was already old before he was born.

Eugene maintains that he wouldn't take a thousand dollars to have a cottonwood in his yard in town, because of the fluff that it would send down onto the roof and into his gutters and onto his pickup. Cottonwoods and magnolias are pretty enough to look at, Eugene says, and good shaders, but aren't worth the raking and cleaning of all those rotting blossoms and wispy cotton balls.

He looks at the black silhouette of the big tree, considering a lifetime of watching its discharge float down like snow. A pleasing sight. And, in spite of his friend's utilitarian notion, entirely worth the trouble. What else, he figures, is stepping out into a new day every morning and putting one foot in front of the other one and getting on with it but dealing with things that might not be worth the trouble. Taking the bad with the good. The chaff with the wheat. The sickness with the health.

He'll go in to bed soon, in the room he was born in, and try to finish the novel he's been reading that he picked up on his last trip down to Houston. It's a good one, and he'd like to see how it comes out, to see if all the loose ends get tied up nicely.

That happens sometimes, he knows. In novels.

The little harbinger commenced its telegraphing not long ago, so persistently that he considers going in and taking one of his pills. Not yet, he decides. Maybe not at all. Let it keep on singing. Its song isn't an unpleasant one, or entirely unwelcome. Just uncomfortable for a time.

There was a piece in the paper this morning about a woman who lived to be a hundred and thirteen years old. He read it all the way through, wondering if she had seen any advantage to such a feat. But the only quote ascribed to her had to do with how much she had always liked chocolate. Nothing about what she had learned, or what she had seen and done. Not one single thing about any difference she had made in all that time. There was a photograph of her, frail and shriveled, being held upright in her bed, staring absently at the camera.

What would be the use of that, he wonders, for the seventh or eighth time since he read the article. Of just hanging on and on, the loose ends of your life dangling always before you.

Just enough of a breeze works through the giant cottonwood to make a few of the stars blink on and off among its leaves. Black woods, quiet and still, lay all around him, beyond the yard and the pastures. In a few days, rifle shots that he won't hear will echo through them in the early mornings and late afternoons. Hunters after deer.

Now . . . there!

One far away honk somewhere in the night. He leans forward in the swing, strains to hear. There's another, then some more, all so high up that he probably wouldn't be able to find them even in daylight. But that's all right, he figures, settling back into the swing for a while longer. They're out there, scurrying along in front of what is pushing them.

Of what is finally coming.

two

the batching plant

i

"So, Boss," Luis asked him one day. "Is this what it will always be for you?"

He moved the tip of his index finger in a wide, high circle, to encompass the entire cement batching plant. He called the other man boss in spite of the fact that he was a decade older, and in spite of the fact that the younger man was in no way his superior. He sometimes called white men that he liked boss, and other Hispanics, *Paco*. This was when he was in a playful mood. Will had never seen him playful enough to address the several Negroes they worked with by anything other than their names. Or Lancaster, the white foreman who *was* their boss; or Cobble, who was also white but was generally considered to be a son of a bitch.

"Is this the American Dream for you?"

Will continued to shovel gravel into the batcher. The pebbles rattled loudly against the metal and sent up a fine, white dust that boiled out of the clatter and over the top of the batcher and settled slowly down on everything. On the pavement under the batching tower. On the truck that was waiting to be filled. On the men that worked in the yard. The white dust lingered always in the yard, and any movement at all brought it to life. Men walking caused it to swirl around their boots and their khaki work pants. Whenever one of the heavy mixer trucks groaned into the yard the dust splashed up around it. A few minutes later, when the truck left to deliver its load of fresh, warm concrete somewhere in Houston, the dust rolled along with the big tires, then followed the truck a ways down Lyons Avenue, like a dog chasing a car.

Will swatted at the dust with his gloved hand.

"I don't have any dream," he said, stabbing a pile of gravel with his shovel. The pebbles ground and sparked against the blade; he spat out some gritty saliva. "All I have is a paycheck."

Luis smiled. The perfect white teeth that were his trademark gleamed, even in the dust that floated around him. He lifted his head up now as he constantly did, as if trying to expand his short, stocky body into its loftiest possible extension, or perhaps attempting to see the world a little better above the white dust. His job was to keep the pile of gravel that the younger man was digging into supplied.

"Boss," he said, clicking his tongue against the white teeth. He shook his head. "Boss, Boss, Boss." He leaned against the shovel now and pulled a heavy work glove tighter on to his hand with the other one. "A man has to have a dream bigger than a paycheck." His English was heavily accented, with sharp, quick stresses falling unexpectedly on random syllables.

Lancaster, the foreman, shouted up at them from the yard.

"Ain't neither one of you girls gonna *have* no goddamn paycheck if you don't get them shovels workin'." All the words mumbled around the cheap cigar that he kept lodged in the corner of his mouth. He never lit the cigar, but gnawed slowly away at it until it finally became so short that it had to be replaced. And so it was that three or four King Edwards gradually retreated into Lancaster's face in the course of each day.

He kept looking up until the two had recommenced the shoveling, watched them for a minute, then ambled over to the dispatcher's shed.

"Someday," Luis said, as he bore down on the spade. "I'll be the one writing the paychecks." And there, encapsulated for perhaps the tenth time that day, was his hope and his salvation. His mantra. His American Dream.

He wiped the sweat from his brow with a wide, fire engine red bandana, then rubbed it several times along the back of his neck. He drove the shovel down into the gravel.

"Me," Luis told the young man, who was already nodding at what he knew was coming, "I'll be writing the checks, you see. And *signing* them. And sitting at a desk in an office with one of the . . . aer . . . aero . . ."

"Air conditioners," Will finished for him, not looking up from his work. Luis nodded, not looking up from his.

From the tower they could see most of the neighborhood. They could see the bakery across the street that specialized in Mexican pastries. Sometimes men went into the bakery early, before going to their jobs, and bought the fruit- or sausage-filled *empanadas,* still warm from the ovens. Then, for the rest of the morning, women and their small children went there, coming out with bags full to brimming of *campechanas* and *novias* and bread or tortillas. Luis went over there occasionally, since he was especially fond of the sweet bread, *Pan de Huevo,* that he said the baker had a way with. Luis shared it with the young man, pulling away big chunks of it, still steaming and yeasty. He had offered some of it to Lancaster, the foreman, only once, and had been laughed at and told that he wasn't studying any Mescin bread and would make do with white.

Beside the bakery were two clapboard houses with unpainted front porches and small grassless yards swept as clean as floors. Negroes of various ages spilled into and out of the houses all day long. Will sometimes wondered if some sort of business was being conducted in the houses, but the Negroes never came out with anything that looked like purchases so he finally had determined that they all must live there. An ancient Negro man sat in a canebacked rocking chair on one of the porches all day every day, in every season, drinking water from a tall glass. Will thought for a while that he might be drinking vodka or gin, but he didn't think that anyone could drink that much vodka or gin and stay upright, even in a chair. The old man never read. Or slept. Or listened to the radio. The people who went into and out of the houses never paid him any attention, nor he them. He sometimes nodded at people who walked along Lyons Avenue, but didn't strike up any conversations. He went into the house periodically to refill the glass and then, doubtless, to relieve himself of its contents.

Past the two houses was a pawn shop owned by a white man, a grocery store owned by a Negro, a couple of more houses and then a gasoline station that employed a mechanic who was sometimes drunk and sometimes sober and never, drunk or sober, a very good mechanic to begin with. A liquor store sat beside the gas station, which must have been handy, Will thought, for the mechanic. The liquor store had the name of its owner on a sign over the door, but all of the men who worked in the concrete plant called it the hooch shop. And much of their weekly paychecks went either there or to one or another of the several honky-tonks farther down the street. Sometimes the prostitutes who worked Lyons Avenue came into possession of some of the men's paychecks and then, consequently, the doctor who practiced two blocks away often benefited also. For they weren't very clean prostitutes.

The hooch shop had been robbed one late afternoon a few weeks before. Will and Luis had watched the thief make a frantic, zigzag escape down as far as the two clapboard houses, where the old Negro on the porch commenced enough of a high-pitched caterwauling to splash water out of his glass and to cause the robber to hesitate long enough for the owner of the hooch shop to catch up close enough to shoot him. The dispatcher at the concrete yard had then called the police, who eventually showed up. But the man was dead. Will and Luis and the other workers and drivers had gone over there and looked at the gaping hole in the man and the pistol that had caused it that the owner of the liquor store waved around, all the while delivering a diatribe about the shallow water sunsuh-bitches and assholes that he had to deal with. Finally an ambulance had come to take the dead thief away, the policemen had talked for a while with the man who had killed him, and everyone had gone back to work at the concrete plant. Three prostitutes had headed off toward the fleabag hotel where they trafficked their wares. The mechanic had gone back to the gas station. The owner of the hooch shop had carefully counted his recovered money as he walked away, as if the dead thief might have managed to smuggle some of it into the next life. The old Negro had settled himself back into his rocker with a fresh glass of water. Then a city bus had bounced to a loud, hissing stop, and several Negro women climbed heavily down in their white maid uniforms, looking wide-eyed at the commotion that had all but completely died away, wanting to know what the hell had happened.

The tall downtown buildings rose up not too many blocks behind the floating white dust of the concrete plant. And then, beyond them, there were nicer places than Lyons Avenue. There was River Oaks, where moneyed people lived in sprawling houses and where the women in the white uniforms worked. Then there were tree-lined streets and handsome buildings where people Will's age went to college at Rice University. And, farther out, beyond Hermann Park and the zoo, there was the new Shamrock Hotel, where big bands played and entertainers like Frank Sinatra sang and rich, pretty girls drank cocktails beside a swimming pool as big as a football field.

Out there, on the other side of the tall buildings, were places that the young man couldn't see from the batching tower of the concrete yard.

✣

Now here was Cobble, leaning against the batching tower. His shirt, at least one size too small, stretched tight against the bulging muscles of his arms and his chest and across his stomach, which leaned out over his belt buckle like an awning over a porch.

"Make 'em sing, *hombres,*" he called up to them. "Make them scoops sing out like a hat dance."

Cobble had as little regard for Mexicans as he did for Negroes. If his worldview had been larger, he would have also hated Jews, Catholics, and any number of other races, religions, and philosophies. But Cobble's base of knowledge was as limited as his vocabulary, so it kept his disdain reined in. He did hate President Truman, he said often and loudly, because he had fired General McArthur. He was a big fan of General McArthur.

"Ever been to one of them hat dances, Martinez?" he said to Luis. He took a swig from his Coca-Cola. Morning sunlight reflected off his sweaty, red scalp, in full view under his close-cropped hair. And off a tall lower incisor, one of the few survivors of what once might have been a full set.

Luis kept at his work.

"You know what the hell I'm talkin' about," Cobble said. He looked at Will, who wasn't a Mexican, but was standing close enough to one to be suspect. "With one of them big ol'—what the hell you call 'em . . . *sombreros*—on the ground. And then all them hot little *muchachas* start bouncing around it. Like jumpin' beans, I guess."

He looked up at Luis through squinted eyes. Rubbed the cool bottle against his neck, then tilted it up and drank off the last of the soda. Belched.

"You mean you ain't never seen them little señoritas do the hat dance down there?" He tilted the bottle in the general direction of the south, in a non-specific prod that might indicate anything from the next block to the South American continent.

Luis stopped shoveling now and looked down at him.

"I guess I never did," he said.

Cobble laughed, as loudly as he had burped. He pointed the empty Coca-Cola bottle at Luis.

"Well, now that's just a damn shame, I'd say." He looked around, to make sure that other workers were watching and listening. He was awfully big on making sure he was being watched and listened to. "I hear tell them little señoritas work up a pretty good sweat in that particular dance." He winked. "Get themselves a little bothered."

Luis continued to look at him. Continued to lean on the shovel. He wiped the back of his stubby neck with his bandana.

"I never saw it," he finally said.

Cobble bounced the empty bottle in his hand and tilted his head just a little.

"I hear tell that you're draggin' this one off to one of your dances," he said, pointing the bottle up at Will. Not much happened in the batching plant that Cobble didn't know about.

Luis had made the invitation many times, telling him that there was more to life than just drinking too much beer in honky-tonks. Telling him that he and his girl would like for him to come along one week and listen to the music, and eat, and laugh, and maybe even dance a time or two with a cousin who was a nice girl from back home who was too damned good for most of the sorry devils who leered at her. Just for a little fun, he had told him.

Luis looked down at Cobble. He was still in the translating process that had to take place in his head when Will moved a little closer to the edge of the platform.

"He's asked me," he said, taking off his cap and rubbing some sweat away from his jaw with it. "What about it?"

Cobble looked up at him through his squinted eyes. A tattooed anchor and chain on his hairy forearm glistened in the sunlight.

"Ain't nothing' about it, son," he finally said. "Just seems a little odd that you'd be wantin' somethin' like that. You bein' . . . so quiet, and all."

He laughed again, and so did some of the other workers.

"You know what I can't figure," he said, tapping the Coca-Cola bottle lightly against his head, "is what you're doin' here at all. You're a big ol' strappin' boy. Appear to be healthy enough." He looked at the other men, like a prosecutor would look at a jury. "When I was your age I was just comin' home from the big war. My mama had to sign me up, 'cause I was just sixteen." He growled out something between a gurgle and a laugh. "Now you're prob'ly thinkin' she just wanted to get shut of me. And that might be right enough. But I sure enough knew where I needed to be, where my duty was." He stepped forward now, planting his two huge boots solidly, causing some of the white dust to boil up around them. He jabbed emphatically toward the street, as if the entire war had been played out specifically in the Mexican bakery on Lyons Avenue.

"Fightin' *Japs!*" He hurled out the words with a confidence that indicated that McArthur had sent for him personally.

He looked at Luis again.

"Now, I guess I know why Martinez here ain't been called up."

His gaze was hard now, directed at the young man.

"But I just can't figure why a big ol' white boy like you got passed by." He bounced the bottle in his hand, then lifted the top close to that one lower tooth. He blew a deep, hollow note.

"Maybe he just ain't been called up," one of the workers said. He looked around at the others. "I ain't been called up."

Cobble looked at the boy who had spoken, then back up at Will. He seemed to be thinking about it.

"Maybe," he said. "And maybe a rich daddy pulled a string or two and figured his baby boy would be better off shovelin' rocks in a batcher and watchin' little señoritas dance than gettin' shot at by the

Koreans." He said Koreans the way he said police, with all of the emphasis on the first syllable.

The young man moved forward on the tower. Luis grabbed his arm, held it tight.

"And maybe I'm just mindin' my own damn business," Will said.

Cobble grinned now. Clenched his big fist tight around the bottle.

"Maybe," he finally said.

A mixer truck rumbled up under the batcher. Cobble laughed again, winked at some of the men, and walked away. The white dust thrown up by the truck floated up to the platform on the tower.

Luis's eyes became not much more than slits in his brown face. The narrow mustache that the young man called his Clark Gable twitched just a little. He stretched his short frame as tall as he could. "Boss," he said, "I think I'm going to have to . . ."

"You ain't going to do *nothing,*" the young man said, over the loud engine of the truck. "How long you think it would take that bastard to turn you in for not having your papers?" He put his cap back on. Adjusted it so that the bill was low over his eyes. "Then you'd be in a hell of a fix. You and all your family you've brought up here."

Will looked at him now. Gave a short tug on the red bandana tied around his neck. Punched his shoulder twice.

"It don't matter," Will said. "It don't matter one bit." He pushed his shovel down into the pile.

More trucks rattled into the yard and then out again on to Lyons Avenue, keeping the blanket of white dust always moving, lifting up in places like a big blanket that the wind had gotten under, then slowly settling back down, until another truck agitated it.

The old Negro, on his porch across the street, watched the movement of the dust, and of the men who worked in it. He drank some of his water, and listened to the clattering of the shovels against the gravel and to the heavy contents of the trucks being turned over in their rollers. He listened to the great engines either idling or harrumphing up enough strength to get themselves going. He rocked slightly and hoped that tomorrow wasn't Sunday. The old Negro was rarely certain what day it was, except on Sunday, when the batching plant was locked up and as still and quiet as something that had died.

And he preferred it to be alive.

On Saturday, Will bathed and put on his only suit and tie and ate the mediocre supper prepared by the woman who owned the boarding house. Then he walked in the late afternoon heat to the meeting hall of the Catholic church that Luis had told him to go to. He got there early, so he waited out on the street and smoked a cigarette and watched everyone as they went in. They were all Mexicans, of course, and they watched him as closely as he watched them. The young, dark men shifted their eyes in his direction through narrow slits; the girls on their arms nodded quickly and then looked down at their print dresses or at the pavement.

"You came, Boss," Luis said when he got there, slapping him on his back. "Good. Good." He waved at a couple of the men and pushed him along in front of him through the doors. "That's good."

The interior of the church hall was all light-colored wood and dull tiles. There were no drapes or blinds on the windows, but each glass pane had been caked over with thick white paint, into which a few drops of yellow tint had been stirred as a small concession to aesthetics. The bare light bulbs on the ceiling reflected in the many rectangles of yellowish white, making it appear that the world outside was bathed in a strange, garish glow. Three crucifixes hung on the walls, all of a suffering Christ, as opposed to a risen one.

Tables along one wall held pastries from the Mexican bakery

across the street from the concrete plant. And there was a large punch bowl filled with red liquid as vibrant as the window panes. Most of the girls held the tiny, chipped cups full of punch, but the boys and men didn't. Will figured that they were either relying on something stronger that they had stashed somewhere outside or wanted to be thought to be doing so.

In a few minutes Luis saw who he had been craning his stout neck to locate and pressed his way through the crowd to get to them. The taller of the two girls met him in the middle of the room and let herself be swallowed up in his bear-like embrace; long black hair fluttered around her big shoulders and she laughed against his face, a loud, commanding laugh that surged across the room like electricity. The other girl, not as tall, held on to her white purse with both small hands in front of her and watched them. When Luis had released the taller one, the other one leaned forward just far enough to receive his quick kiss on her cheek.

Luis waved the young man over, and his name became quickly lost in the hurried business of introductions. "Maria," Luis said, nodding slightly in the direction of the taller one.

"Mary," she said.

"And this is Estella," Luis said.

"Stella," Mary said.

The shorter girl looked just briefly up at Will.

"*Estella,*" she said, still holding tight to her purse, speaking so low that it was barely intelligible in the general hubbub of young people anxious for the dance that was about to begin.

The music started up, provided by a *conjunto* made up of three musicians and a girl of seventeen or so who held a tambourine. There was an accordionist, who bore the brunt of the melody, a guitarist, and a drummer.

The first number was a lively one, setting the crowd into frantic motion. The accordion rang out in sharp blasts, and Will heard occasionally a series of *yip, yip yip's* that didn't seem to come from anyone or anywhere in particular, but from the bouncing mass itself.

Luis and Mary quickly found two chairs against the wall for the other two to sit in, got a cup of the red punch for Estella, and then made their way to the dance floor.

Will looked first at the dancers, then at the *conjunto,* then at his shoes that could have stood a bit more polish and effort than they had been given, then at this girl sitting beside him. Her hair was dark and long, though not as dark or as long as Mary's. It wasn't done up and pinned down like the young man's mother's hair or the woman who owned the boarding house, but fell loosely beside her face. She was nineteen, like him, Luis had told him. She wore a white dress with a flower and vine design and, in spite of the heat, a light sweater draped over her shoulders.

They were pretty shoulders, he suspected, though all he had to base his judgment on was a pretty face and neck. She was not as dark as Luis and Mary, more a light brown, like just a drop or two of chocolate folded into a bowl of rich cream. And she wasn't as big as Mary, who he suspected was one of those girls who would only get bigger. But not this girl, he knew. She would always be small. Not like his mother, who was small and hard, in her body and her eyes and her disposition. But . . . delicate, he thought. Delicate. He might have nodded at the assessment. He realized suddenly that it must be obvious he was staring at her.

"I doubt you'll be needing that sweater tonight," he said.

She nudged her shoulders up, pulled at a small imitation pearl button.

"I just wore it," she said.

They sat quietly for a few minutes, and most of the people in the room kept stealing glances at them. He felt awkward being in such a large gathering of only Mexicans and felt the first nudge of resentment at Luis for getting him into such a predicament. He wished he was at a honky-tonk, drinking beer. He looked at the girl again.

His experience with women had been limited, having had no sisters or cousins from which to learn their peculiar ways. He'd been on a few dates in high school, one of which had ended up in the back seat of the girl's father's Buick in a poorly choreographed rolling around that might or might not have been sex. He had never been in anything that could have been even remotely considered a relationship and had never been to any of the prostitutes with other men who worked at the batching plant.

"Did you grow up in Houston?"

He must have still been staring at her. At the creamy smoothness of her neck. At the most delicate and perfectly curling dark eyelashes that he had ever seen. It occurred to him that he'd almost certainly never paid any attention at all to eyelashes—his own or anyone else's—but he couldn't seem to pull his attention away from these.

"Did you grow up in Houston?" she said again.

She was leaning closer to him now. Her accent was as heavy as Luis's; she managed to start Houston with a *u* rather than an *h*.

He shook his head. Looked at the dancers again. He told her he grew up in the country, on a little farm, that he had come here just for the work and to live in a bigger place for a while.

"I don't guess you grew up here either," he said.

She took a sip from her punch, barely touching the edge of the cup to her lips. Shook her head.

"I grew up in the county, too," she said. "In Mexico." She pronounced it the way Luis did, making it a prettier sound than he had always heard. "I came here with Maria." She patted at the edge of her mouth with the napkin she was holding. "With Mary."

He asked if she wanted some more of the punch, and she said she didn't. So they watched the dancing again for a long minute or two.

"I like the country better," she said. "Do you?"

He was looking at her dark eyes again and at those eyelashes.

"I like them both about the same, I guess," was the best that he could come up with.

The second of the fast songs came to an end now, and the dancers all applauded and yipped and laughed, the tall girl's loud laugh rising above all of it. Then the girl holding the tambourine started singing a ballad in Spanish, her voice soft and mellow and almost too small for the gasping accordion that was her accompaniment. The couples moved slowly, the rhythm of each pair becoming just one swaying movement, floating in perfect sync with the music and the sound of the girl's voice.

"We could dance to that one, I guess," Will said.

Estella put the cup down on the chair beside hers. Then she nodded, and, not looking at each other, they got up and stepped through the crowd.

He had never danced before, but he had watched it being done plenty of times at the honky-tonks. He had learned how to dispose of a wasp nest with a burning newspaper by watching it being done, and how to drive a pickup, so there wasn't any reason, he figured, that he couldn't take up dancing just as easily.

He cupped her small hand in his, as carefully as he might lift up the absolute runt of a litter of new born pups, and touched her side with just the tips of his fingers. Estella touched his side with the small purse that she still held tightly, and they moved gracelessly around for a moment, as if trying to avoid stepping into puddles in a pathway.

"I'm not too good at it," he said, trying hard not to step on her toes.

She said that she thought he was and nodded to emphasize that she was sincere. Then he stepped on her toes, and she grimaced.

"I'm not very good, either," she said.

When the song ended, they went back to their chairs with Luis and Mary and soon they were left alone again while the other two danced. It didn't take long for them to establish that she worked at the place that Luis had found for her and Mary, on the packaging line at the Nabisco plant. That she liked to go to the movies because she liked the stories, and because they helped her to learn English faster. That he enjoyed movies too, especially anything with John Wayne in it, and that he thought she spoke English just fine. That he liked the name Estella.

"Mary says it's not American enough. She wants me to use Stella."

She smoothed out the folds of her dress. Touched the pearl button of her sweater.

"I like Estella better," he said.

And she smiled at him for the first time.

The next song was another slow one, and they danced to it. He was a little more confident now, a little more at ease. She leaned closer to him this time; her dark hair touched the side of his face, and he could smell the sweetness of it. Her hand was soft and small in his, and he could feel her other hand resting nicely on his back. The music floated along and so did they, and Will figured that this was more than likely an important night. An important moment.

He figured, after just under two hours in her presence, that he was done for now.

It started raining on Sunday afternoon and it was still raining on Monday morning when Will went to work. It rained off and on for most of the week, making the work in the batching plant a wet, slushy business but, at least, rendering the floating white dust less of a nuisance.

He and Luis spoke only once of the dance, when Luis said that Estella had enjoyed it and that he was glad that the young man had seen that there hadn't been any hopping around a sombrero. They ate their lunch of *Pan de Huevo* and sausage *empanadas* that Luis had bought at the bakery across the street.

"I was thinking that I might come down there again," Will said, paying close attention to the hot bread that he pulled apart. "Sometime."

Luis looked at him now. He laid his half-eaten *empanada* back into its brown paper.

It had stopped raining, but the dark, summer clouds hung so low and heavy that the tops of the tall buildings were hidden. Drops of dirty water fell off the tower and plopped into puddles around them.

"Boss," Lewis said. He made a crease in the brown paper, then slid it through his fingers. Will watched him.

"Estella is my pri . . . , my cousin, you know."

Will nodded, then looked at his boots. He kicked gently at some of the mud and gravel.

"I'm just talking about dancing," he said.

"I know you are, Boss. And there's nothing wrong with dancing. I, you know . . ." He was struggling now, the young man knew. Weighing the words before he used them, not at all sure they were the right ones. "I brought Estella here, you know. With Maria. Our village was not a . . ." He searched harder now, the lines over his dark eyes becoming deeper furrows at the work. "It was a small . . . *town.*" He relaxed a little, satisfied with the result.

"Well," Will said, "I guess I know that. I'm from a little town myself."

"That's right," Luis said. "But Estella, she's never been anywhere before. And she misses her *madre.*"

"Her mother."

"Yes. Her mother."

A low, rumbling of thunder rolled slowly through the dark clouds. Someone honked their car horn on Lyons Avenue. The young man looked across the street at the old Negro man in his rocking chair on his porch, gazing up at the clouds and drinking some of his water.

"Estella, you see," Luis went on, "she's never been anywhere but here, and back in that . . . town. And she is very . . . *inocente.*"

"Innocent," Will said. "Well, Luis, I don't mean to . . ."

"I know that Boss," Luis said, tapping his arm. "I know that." He smiled, his white teeth brilliant even in the shade of the tower on a rainy day. "I know that. I just don't want . . . I don't . . ."

Will ate the last of his lunch. Sucked the last crumbs of sausage from his fingers. Wiped his hands on his shirt.

"You don't want her to get hurt."

Luis nodded at that. Then he fixed his attention for a long time on the paper he still held.

A mixer truck turned off Lyons Avenue into the yard and lumbered up beside them, bouncing heavily to a stop. In not too many minutes, they were back on the tower, shoveling gravel into the batcher, both of them knowing, without saying it out loud, that something had changed. That something was different now. Something that included a wider distance, and excluded dancing in church halls.

The rain started up again that afternoon, slowly at first and, a few minutes before the five o'clock whistle blew on top of the dispatcher's shed, a little harder. The last truck had been filled and had groaned away, and they climbed down off the tower, their ponchos soaked and dripping.

"Well, *hombres,*" Cobble said, finding a dry Lucky Strike in his pocket and lighting it, "I hear tell somebody finally got him a look-see at the old hat dance."

Several of the workers grouped around. One of them laughed. No doubt, Will thought, the one who had told him. He had probably been there.

"I hear tell," Cobble went on, taking a long pull on the cigarette and breathing out the next words with the smoke, "that somebody turns out to have a taste for . . . *tamale.*"

Luis was out of his poncho now; he tossed it down to the ground. Will pushed him aside and stepped forward.

"I guess you're talking about me," he said, moving up close him. "So why don't you just say it to me."

Cobble flicked the cigarette away. Pushed the last of the smoke down through his black nostrils. It was raining harder now, splashing into the puddles in the yard and spilling off the tower and the men themselves.

"Well, I ain't called no names," he almost mumbled, growling it out low like the thunder they had been hearing all day, "but if you're the tamale eater, I guess you're who I need to talk to."

He hadn't had any experience at fighting, and his first punch was blocked by Cobble's thick forearm. The big man pummeled him solidly, just once, on the side of his face. Then he watched him for a few seconds, looked at the other men, smiled a snarling grin that said that this would be no chore at all. That this would be small potatoes.

Will reached up and wiped away some of the blood that had appeared at his nose and knew, without any need for verification, that a tooth was loose. Or gone.

Cobble anchored himself with his stout legs, clenching his big fists into what looked, to the young man, like mallets.

"How'd ya like it?" he growled. The other workers had gathered closer around them now in the rain. A few of them laughed. "That little tamale taste pretty good?" He stepped closer. "Was it spicy?" He laughed along with the men. "Was it sorta sweet?"

His head reeled; he had to stagger to keep his balance. Luis moved forward beside him, but he pushed him back again. Some of the other Mexicans held him now. They all watched the young man fall against Cobble, hurling punches up into the broad face as swiftly as he could. The big man pushed some of them aside, but one or two landed solid, just not solid enough to move him.

By the time it was over, and Cobble had been pulled away by Lancaster, the foreman, and Luis had still been held back by several of the Mexicans, and Will lay curled up in the muddy yard, Lancaster stood in the hard rain and yelled out the settlement.

"This here is *done!*" the foreman shouted. He pointed down at the ground, then stabbed in its direction three or four times. "This here is over with!" He looked around at everybody assembled in the group; removed the soggy King Edward that had been clamped in his mouth and threw it away from him. Cobble stood with his huge hands on his hips, a single trickle of blood working its way slowly down his red face.

"Anybody that thinks it ain't done," Lancaster shouted, "can see me! And I don't handle shit like this with my fists." He pointed at the entrance to the yard. "I handle it by sending you out that goddamned gate once and for all." He leaned down and picked up his hat, which had somehow ended up in the mud during the skirmish. He tried to wipe some of the mud off, and slapped it twice against the side of his leg.

"There ain't one more goddamned thing going to be said or done about this here," Lancaster said, not shouting now. But still loud enough for all to hear it clearly. "Here in this yard or anywhere else. And if I learn different, then we'll have us a vacancy." He nodded at that. Spat. "Sure enough."

He put the dripping, misshapen hat back on, pulled a soaked handkerchief out of his back pocket, and wiped his hands as clean as he could manage.

"Now all of you get the hell on away from here."

He walked toward the dispatcher's shed. Stopped. Looked at Cobble.

"You got any questions?" he said.

Cobble glared at him through his squinted eyes. A blue-black bruise was already rising beside one of them.

"I don't figure I . . ." the big man started.

"I don't figure you *do,*" the foreman finished for him. He stepped a little closer. "Because this here is over with."

Later, when Luis had gotten him to his feet and walked with him in the rain to his small, rented house several blocks from Lyons Avenue, when Mary had yelped long and loudly about people getting beatings, even in America, then had washed the cuts and bruises with iodine and alcohol, when Luis had heated up some soup full of vegetables and pepper and made him eat it and drink some brandy from a jelly jar, Estella sat beside him and ran her slender fingers through his hair.

She cried just a little, the tears glistening in those eyelashes, and said some words that he didn't understand. He looked at the eyelashes and the dark eyes and the small nose that had been his undoing and reached up and touched her soft, dark hair and the creamy skin beside her mouth.

Then, just before the brandy took its effect, Luis was back, saying that he looked better already, and calling him Boss, and telling him that what he needed was some dancing Friday night, down at the church hall. That would do it. That that would fix him up.

Then there was just Estella, before he fell asleep, with the taste of the sweet brandy still in his mouth, mixed with the spices from the soup and some blood from his loose tooth.

Estella. Smiling for him again. Not crying now, but just sitting quietly beside him in the dim light of the one lamp in the room.

ii

"So, you've fallen in with Mexicans," is what his mother had to say about it.

He had arrived the previous night, on Christmas Eve, on the Greyhound bus that provided his rare journeys north. His father had met him at the café that served as the bus station in town, then not more than a dozen words had been employed on the way out to the little farm in the pickup that had belonged to their father and grandfather. They had smoked while they waited for the bus driver to pull his suitcase from the luggage compartment and they smoked again during the short trip in the pickup. Skeletons of trees had come out of the cold night into the illumination of the headlights, then had slid slowly back into darkness. Will had rubbed his hands together and pulled his jacket tight, for the heater hadn't worked in years.

His father had said that it was mighty cold. Only that.

Now here was morning and the overwarm parlor and the sparse, tilted cedar in the corner hung sporadically with glass ornaments and cellophane wrapped candy canes from the five and dime in town. His mother looking not very comfortable on the same worn chair that she had looked not very comfortable on for as long as he could remember. The sky a gun metal gray outside the windows.

What he had wanted to tell her was that he had fallen in love with this girl. Had fallen head over heels in love for the first and only time in his life and that it had knocked the wind completely out of him, like the time he had fallen out of the cottonwood tree out there in the yard. But he never could have told her something like that, of course, so he had simply reported the facts of the matter.

"And you're sure about it?" she said. She tapped her spoon lightly against the porcelain cup and saucer that she was holding. "Sometimes they say that just to catch a boy up."

What he had intended to tell her—he had worked the words through his mind on the bus the night before, polishing them, sometimes whispering them—was that he had never been through anything like this. Had never met anybody like this girl and had never felt as comfortable around another human being as he did around her. Which would have been a lie, he knew. Since there had been one other person that he had been that comfortable with. That sure of.

"I'm sure about it," he said. He was trying to see up that slight hill to the big pasture, but the morning fog was too thick to make out anything past the board fence at the edge of the yard.

He had known all along that he would have to tell her that she was a Mexican, and he had determined that the best way to convey something like that would be at the beginning. So he had rattled it out last night after supper, when his father had gone out to the porch to smoke. It had been a rapid accounting that had been nothing like what he had planned, the pertinent facts rising like globs of heavy cream in the separator.

"And how do you know it's yours?" She almost smiled now. "Did you ever think about that?"

He watched his father through the window. Watched the big man move slowly around in the cold morning, the massive, bare framework of the cottonwood stretching up over him into the fog, like some carefully put together edifice whose entire exterior has fallen away. He dug around for something in the wide toolbox in the bed of the pickup and smoked his cigarette. Tobacco and candle smoke perturbed her allergies. So there wasn't any smoke allowed in the house other than what might be occasionally blown back out of the fireplace on a blustery day.

"I don't need to think about it," he said. "It's mine."

So there it was. As exposed now, in the tepid room, as the socks and undershirts and boxes of cheap drugstore candy that lay beside the wrappings that had contained them.

"And you intend to marry her." She put the cup and saucer down on the side table. Folded her arms. "Is that what you said?"

The clanging around that his father was doing in the toolbox came sharp and loud through the cold morning. He finally found what he was searching for and lifted it out. Looked at it. Wiped some of the early morning dampness from it with his hand. Laid it on the sideboard. Then he let the lid of the box slam shut, leaned over it, smoked his cigarette, and looked out into the fog.

"Yes, m'am," he said. "I surely do."

Now they both sat quietly. He kept looking out the window; she looked at him. The big radio that he used to listen to with the old man still sat in the same place. But it wasn't turned on. His father had said, last night, that one of the television sets he had seen at a store in Tyler would have made a nice Christmas present for the family. And she had been quick to say that they were ugly pieces of furniture, in her opinion, and that that glass eye staring at her all day would bother her. That she'd stick with the radio for her entertainment. And books from the library.

"It hasn't even occurred to you, has it?" she said. "That you played right into her hands. And more than likely her family's."

She leaned forward on the sofa. Pointed at him.

"People like that see a boy like you as a ticket." She nodded. "Can't you see that? As just a way to get their papers." She nodded again, then made a little ticking sound to show how silly he'd been. "That never occurred to you?"

His father was still leaning against the pickup, one boot hitched on the running board. He nudged the thing he had dug out of the toolbox—the young man could make it out now; a fence wire stretcher—a few inches out of his way. He rocked a little against the truck, the small, filterless cigarette almost lost between two thick fingers. He spat tiny bits of tobacco out, then pinched a few more from his lower lip with the same hand he held the cigarette in and flicked them away.

"You know what he'll think about it," his mother said. "Don't you?"

He knew.

"It don't matter how he thinks," he said, more quickly than either of them had expected. He turned toward her. "It don't matter what you think."

She leaned back against the cushion.

"Is that right?" She used one small hand to press the edge of her sweater against the sofa. "Well, that's just fine."

She slid her palm along the sweater as if she were ironing it.

"That's a fine way to look at it."

"It doesn't have anything to do with you," he said. "With neither one of you. I don't live here anymore."

"We do," she said. It was neither loud nor particularly quiet. It was an emotionless declaration of a simple reality.

"We have to live here. We have to go sit in that Baptist Church every Sunday morning where everybody we know can look at us. I have to shop at the stores in town, and at the Piggly Wiggly in Tyler where half the town always is. And your daddy likes to go to the feed store and sit around the heater with the other men. And what do you think the topic of conversation will be now, when he gets up and leaves?"

He could blurt out something now, he knew. About it not making a damned bit of difference what other people thought. But he didn't.

"And I think you know what *he'd* think about it."

He was watching him again, through the window.

"I already . . ."

"Not him," she said.

He looked at her now. Every tick of the clock on the mantle was a small door clanging shut. He could hear some of the dry cedar needles falling through the dead tree and landing on the wood floor.

"Your grandfather never was the saint you made him out to be," she said. She reached over for her cup, tilted it up to assure herself it was either empty or that the coffee in it was cold, dropped it back into its saucer. "Though I might as well knock my head against a wall as tell you that."

He tried something like a smile now.

"He was a Baptist, Mama. I doubt he'd make a saint."

"He didn't even make much of a Baptist. I could count the times he went down there."

His father took a final, long drag on his cigarette, then dropped it and ground it out with his heel. They watched him come up on the porch.

When they'd had the last of the coffee and his father had driven off in the truck to throw some hay out to the cows, he packed the gifts he had received and the brick-shaped pound cake his mother had wrapped in wax paper into his suitcase and sat it by the door. He had to catch the bus at ten.

She was moving the breakfast dishes from the table to the sink. He leaned against the kitchen doorway, his hands in his pockets. He had on the sweater she had knitted that had been the biggest of his presents that morning.

"You're wrong about it," he told her.

His father's plate, and his, hardly needed washing at all. The mopping up they had done with her biscuits had done the job nicely.

"You're wrong about her. And her family."

She scraped what she hadn't eaten from her own plate into the garbage can.

"Her cousin is named Luis. I've told you about him. He's a good man, Mama. He just got married, himself. Not even a month ago."

She was putting things away now. Butter. Fig preserves. He knew that she would normally have done this an hour ago; would have commenced her cleaning up even before he and his father had gotten up from the table. She had been in the parlor all that time. Thinking.

"I wanted to tell you about her," he said. "About how . . ." Why was *wonderful* such a hard word to come by right now, he wondered. Why was *incredible* as useless to him at the moment as any word picked at random from any page in a dictionary.

"She never set out to trap me into this."

He stepped up and rested his hands on the back of one of the straight-backed chairs.

"It just happened. That's all. And now I'm going to make it right." He kicked the chair leg twice, softly, with his shoe. "And you and Daddy will just have to see it. That's all."

She was stirring detergent into the hot water in the dishpan. Stirring it slowly into bubbles. She lifted up a palm full of bluish white foam. Dropped it back to the pan. She turned off the water, stirred the suds around some more.

"There's the religion, too," she said. "If there's anything to this girl, like you say there is, than she'll be too devoted to her church to ever leave it. And that would mean you'd have to become a Catholic."

She breathed out the last part, as if it was something as ludicrous as him attempting to become a horse, or a tree.

She turned quickly now and faced him. Shot out the next words before he could say anything. She had worked it all out, he suspected, in the parlor. Now she intended to deliver it.

"There's things you can do."

He saw something in her eyes now that he had never seen there before. Something frantic, desperate.

"There's a . . . medical thing . . . that you can arrange." Her hands were dripping with the dishwater. "I could help you pay for it. And your daddy would never have to know about it."

She took half a step towards him. Then another one.

"You'd have to ask around. Probably some of the men you work with have had to do it, and they could help you. I'd give you some money."

She was pleading now, he realized. That was the thing in her eyes, in her face. She was begging.

"Or you could just not do anything. Do you know that?"

She nodded her head at that one. This one might be best, the nod said.

"It's not uncommon. It happens all the time, I expect."

She was working her way through her list, he knew. Like a lawyer covering every point. Every angle.

"I mean, they're not Americans. Are they? It's not like they can go to the law. Isn't that right?"

He stared at her now. Let all of it sink in for a moment.

"You're not even thinking of how Estella and me feel about anything," he said. "It seems like what we think about it ought to be the important thing."

She squinted her eyes a little at that. Tilted her head up a fraction of an inch. Let one side of her mouth contort itself into what might, with considerably more effort, become a smile.

"Is that right?"

She reached behind her and found the cup towel. Dried her hands.

"You're both happy, are you? You've had yourselves some fun and now you're ready for the next part. Is that it?"

The desperation was gone now. The frantic groping for options. It had all finally come around right, her gaze said. It was clear now, and she was back to a place where she could see it plainly.

"Now you figure you're ready for the *living* part. Because that's the hard part, I can tell you. The month after month, and then the year after year of not having enough money. Of getting by. And getting old. That's the part that's far and away different from the part that made this baby."

She pulled at the two ends of the little towel.

"And what *about* the baby? And the one after that. And the next one. It hasn't occurred to you, has it, that they won't be American. And they won't be Mexican. They won't be *anything*, as far as most Americans and Mexicans will see it."

"They'll be Americans," he said. "It don't have to be like that."

"Well, that's right," she said. "And I wish it wasn't. But it is. And you know it is."

She waited. Maybe expecting him to say something more. When he didn't, she went on.

"You'll have to live with this a long time. And so will she. Have you thought about that? The years will be just as hard for her. Maybe even harder, since she's the girl. Since she'll be the mother."

He shook his head. Waved his hand.

She watched him for another moment, then turned back to the sink, went back to her work.

He pulled the chair back that he was holding on to and sat down at his place, where he had eaten no telling how many thousands of breakfasts and dinners and suppers. He looked at the empty chair across the table. A cigarette would be fine right now, he thought. A cigarette was what he needed. He reached over and ran the tip of one finger along the tablecloth in front of the empty chair.

"Why did you say that?" he asked. "Before. About him not being a saint?"

She scrubbed at one of the plates that he had eaten from all of his life. That the old man had eaten from. The faded blue cornflower design glistened through the suds.

"There was a woman in town."

"The woman that sold him the peach brandy."

"She *gave* it to him. Not sold. But that wasn't her, anyway. That's not who I'm talking about."

She finished the plate, then laid it on the drain board. Slid the next one into the water.

"He knew her even before your grandmother died. Maybe it started back then. I don't know. There was always some talk."

She studied the plate she was scrubbing. Then scrubbed a little more.

"Then when he was a widower, I think everybody sort of expected him to take up with her. In public. Maybe even marry her."

She took the coffeepot out to the back porch and dumped the grounds into the frozen flower bed. Brought it back to the sink and gave it a good washing.

"Why didn't he?"

She washed it out three times before it passed her inspection. Then she sat it upside down beside the plates. Wiped her hands dry. Folded the cup towel neatly and laid it down. Leaned against the counter. Closed her eyes.

"Because she was a Mexican."

He said it as he might give the answer to an arithmetic problem that he had finally worked out. She kept her eyes shut tight. Nodded.

The morning was brighter now, outside the window over the

sink. A mockingbird pecked persistently at something on one of the boards of the fence.

"I always knew he *wanted* her," she said, still leaning against the counter, looking out her window. "Especially after he was left by himself, in that house where he had lived with your grandmother for so long. Where he had raised your daddy. Men who've been married for a long time don't usually stay by themselves too long after their wife dies. It's different for women. They see it as a sort of . . . relief. As a different way to live. That's why there's so many widows by themselves."

The mockingbird gave up on whatever it was that he was after and flew off.

"When your daddy was off in the war," she said, wiping the curved lip of the sink with a wet rag, "and the three of us lived here, he used to go off in the truck at night. And I knew where he was going."

He looked again at the empty place across from him. Could almost see the tiny porcelain cup being lifted up like a baseball in the huge hand.

"Then, after an hour or so, I'd hear the truck come back, and him trying to be careful not to slam its door. Then he'd sit out on the front porch for the longest time. Not doing anything, I guess. Just looking at the stars, maybe."

She sat down in her own chair now. Heavily. Like he had seen her plop down into it after long days. She clasped her hands together in front of her on the table.

"Sometimes he'd stay out there 'til daylight. Then he'd get up and go on about his business like he did every other morning."

They sat perfectly still. In a little while he heard the old pickup groaning up the hill. His father would have been keeping up with the time, to make sure he got back early enough to get him to town before the bus arrived.

"He *couldn't* have done it," she said. Now she reached over and took both of his hands in hers. She had never done that, that he could remember. It startled him. "Not to your daddy. Don't you see? He couldn't have done something like that and still been the man he held himself up to be."

She squeezed his hands now. Leaned forward. Looked at the door that he would be coming in. Listened as the pickup got closer.

"He couldn't have let your daddy come back home from that war and have people talk about that in town. Don't you see?"

A single tear started just at the edge of her eye. Nothing more than a glisten at first. A twinkle. Then it took on enough of a shape to travel and moved slowly down beside her nose and nestled in the crease at the edge of her mouth.

"He couldn't any more have done that," she said, wiping the tear away, letting go of his hands, waiting for her husband to come up on to the porch and into the house, "than you can do *this.*"

They made quick, bouncing stops at every town along the highway. It was the only Dallas to Houston run that day, but nobody had gotten on or off at any of the gas stations or eateries since Will had boarded. So there were still five of them, including the driver, who wore his pointy Greyhound cap pushed back on his head, and made no attempt to hide either the fact that he was dipping snuff, which he spat into a creamed corn can, or that he wasn't any too happy about having to work on Christmas day. He waited for just long enough at each of the stations to be sure that nobody was either coming or going, then worked the bus through its loud gears out of the deserted little towns. Past closed up hardware and feed stores. Past empty schools and churches. Past house after house full of people keeping their Christmas near heaters and fireplaces.

"Had to leave this mornin' even before the kids rolled out to see what Santy Claus brung 'um," the driver said. He lifted the can up close, shot a solid, pinging dart of tobacco juice into it, then looked in his mirror to make sure the woman three seats behind Will was still sleeping. Two Negro boys sat in the very back, playing cards.

"The old lady didn't even much want to give me my own little Santy Claus present afore I rolled out myself," he said. Winked. Smiled.

Will smiled back, then looked out the frosty window.

They were between towns now. Pastures full of dead grass and cold cattle moved by. Thick pine forests. There were creeks and farmhouses and hay barns. Windmills occasionally. Brick chimneys on some of the houses sent smoke billowing out into the slate colored afternoon.

He would see Estella in an hour or so. He'd walk down to his rooming house from the bus depot and leave his suitcase. Then he'd walk over to Luis's and Mary's and he would see Estella.

He looked at his watch. It had been almost exactly twenty-four hours since he had seen her. One day. And in a little over an hour he would hand her the two Christmas gifts that were in his room.

"This here is the thing," the driver was saying. "There ain't no reason why we ought to be in this here thing at all. I never even knew where Korea *was* 'til we'd got into it. Now here we are in a big ass war"—he glanced at his mirror again, to make sure of the sleeping woman—"not even ten years after we finished the last 'un."

Estella would be waiting for him. She would have made something special probably, it being Christmas. A cake, maybe. Or a pie. She had been practicing her baking.

"I swear," the driver said. He lifted his can up again. Spat. "It seems like we just can't stay out of being in a ruckus somewhere or another. Don't it seem that way to you?"

Will said it did.

He had mentioned just the one time, during a movie they were watching at a big downtown theater, that the pie Doris Day was cutting looked awfully good. And she had asked Mary, who was a good hand at cooking, to teach her.

They had gone to the movies pretty often. He liked westerns best, but she enjoyed the ones set in modern times. Comedies, especially. When she laughed, her eyelashes fluttered in a way that he especially liked, and then she'd look at him to see if he was laughing, too.

"Now if some bunch uh sunsuhbitches was to come over here and attacked us, on our own ground, well, then, I could see the sense in it, then. Hell, I'd go sign up my own self if that was to happen. Even with these flat feet uh mine."

They liked to take the bus out to Hermann Park. Sometimes they rented a paddle boat; sometimes they went through the zoo; sometimes they just walked along, or sat under one of the big trees and talked. About growing up on the farm and about growing up in a small village. About his grandfather. And her mother.

"Far as I can see," the driver was saying, "we ain't got one bit of bidness over yonder. And now that MacArthur's out of it, we ain't likely to win it nohow. So what I say is why don't we just come on the hell *home.*" A little boy in the front seat of a car they met waved at him. He waved back. "Don't you see?"

His father had waved like that at people on the short drive in to town to catch the bus. People in cars and on the sidewalk. He had called out to one of the men. Laughed. Will had watched him as he drove, as he shifted the gears of the old truck. It was too cold for him to rest his arm in the window, as he almost always did. So he had kept it in his lap.

" . . . a no-account bunch, if you was to ask me," the driver was saying now. "Ever last one of um. Republicans, Democrats. What have you."

They had saved up their money a couple of times, and gone dancing at places other than the hall of the Catholic church. At supper clubs that had a professional orchestra and a crooner. Luis and

Mary, newlyweds now, had gone with them the first time, when the man at the door had thought a long few minutes before letting them in. Then they had gone by themselves the second time.

His father had asked him, when they had stopped at the only intersection in town, when he would be coming back up. And he'd told him he didn't know. In the spring maybe. Or the summer. His father had never offered an opinion about his moving down to Houston after he finished high school. He knew that he would have figured that he would have to make his own way. Live his own life.

There had been an abundance of talk about the future among the four of them. Mostly from Luis. "We'll find us a place, Boss," he'd tell him, after a couple of beers, or maybe something a little stronger, "where they'll be needing lots of concrete. And we'll start out with one tower and one truck. We'll get a used truck, you see? Mary and Estella can work in the office and answer the telephone, and you and me, we'll mix the batches and haul them. Then we'll get bigger." He'd smile then and nod a little at the plan. "That's the American Dream," he'd say, almost whispering the words.

" . . . that a new bed was what we need, I kept telling her," the driver was saying. He looked at the sleeping woman in the mirror. Lowered his voice just a little. "On account of the springs in the old un had done wore out." Now he found Will in the mirror. Grinned. "If you get me."

It was after that second visit to a supper club, when they had both had several glasses of not too bad wine, that they had made love for the first time. When Luis and Mary had taken the train down to Galveston for the night. When by candlelight he had first unbuttoned her dress—slowly, fumbling at each button with nervous fingers—and had first touched her in the way that he had imagined for weeks. Then he had watched her sleeping the next early morning, even before daylight when moonlight painted her milk chocolate skin an altogether other color, her head nestled in the crook of his arm.

"But she was dead set on a chester drawers, and that was all there was to that," the driver said. He shifted down one gear to slow down for a stop sign at a crossroads. "So hell, I went down to Sears and Roebuck and put one on the lay away."

The bus had already been pulling off the highway when they had arrived, so his father hadn't gotten out. He had leaned over and shaken his hand, and told him to take good care of himself.

"Make us proud," he had told him.

Then he had pulled the door shut and driven off.

Will looked at the back of the driver's cap. He tried to listen to what he was saying, but then he was thinking of the two gifts again. One was a box of scented bath soaps he'd bought and had wrapped at the McCrory's near the rooming house. The other one was smaller, and since the box itself was covered in fabric, he hadn't worried about getting that one wrapped. It was the least expensive ring in the pawn shop on Lyons Avenue, but the man had sworn that it was a real diamond. Just not very much of one. And he'd told him that it was a quality ring, fine quality gold, that they could add stones on to later. When they could afford it.

Make us proud, his father had said.

An hour later, after they had stopped in two more little towns where no one either entered the bus or left it, Will had worked it all out.

" . . . best way is on top of the stove in a Dutch oven," the driver was saying. But by this time, Will wasn't making any effort whatsoever to follow along.

He couldn't stay at the boarding house tonight; he knew that well enough. Because they expected him back in the city, and Luis would come looking for him. So he'd have to go by there and get what he needed. Maybe he'd sleep in the train station; it wasn't too far away. People slept in depots, he imagined, when they had long waits between trains. He'd need to get at least a little sleep, he knew, since he had no idea how long the process would take tomorrow. So he hoped that nobody would object to him stretching out on one of the benches at Union Station. He'd eat some of the pound cake in his suitcase for his supper, then the rest of it for breakfast. If the process was speedy enough, Uncle Sam could provide his meals after that. Things would be open for business in the morning, and he could be there waiting when the recruiter unlocked his doors.

"Now my mother-in-law," the driver said, "she maintains that the only way is inside a oven. But I swear, all you end up with then is a dry bird."

He'd have to forego the pay he had coming at the batching plant, of course. He couldn't go there. But he guessed he wouldn't need any money for a while.

" . . . old man'll be three sheets to the wind, mor'n likely, by the time we get over there. After I push this here dog all the way back up to Dallas. And her mother'll set a bird on the table that will look like a million bucks. But I'll wager you a dollar to a . . ."

His father had grasped his hand hard when he had shaken it, like his grandfather had always shaken a man's hand. The way he used to watch the old man do it in town, or when a man would come up into the yard under the cottonwood tree. His father had winked at him when he spoke, he thought. Maybe not. But he had said the words. He was sure enough about that.

"Now, I don't give a damn," the driver checked his mirror again; the woman's mouth was wide open now, her head leaning over against the cold window that was as fogged up now as the driver's, "what a bird looks like when it sits on the damn table. That don't matter none to me." He waved one hand back and forth to show how little it mattered to him.

He closed his eyes and hoped that the rocking of the bus and the steady cadence of the driver's voice would lull him into a short nap before they arrived. But Estella's face kept him awake. Those eyelashes and that little bit of a nose. She'd cry a good bit; he was certain of that. Not in front of Mary and Luis, but when she was by herself. And there would be that cake or pie she would have made for him, which she'd have to look at sitting all by itself on the table. That would be a bad business for a little while, until she finally told Luis or Mary to throw it away.

He watched her crying now, then here was his father's big hand coming at him across the pickup seat. Then it was neither of those things, but some sort of combination of both of them. For a few brief seconds, he even saw the old Negro on his porch on Lyons Avenue. Holding his glass of water and watching the batching plant. Wondering why there was only one man up on the tower.

When he opened his eyes, he could just make out the tops of Houston's downtown buildings on the horizon.

"What I want," the driver was saying, leaning up over the wide steering wheel and stretching, "is a bird that's got some juice left in it when I eat it."

He spat again into his corn can. Yawned.

"And I'll grant you, the one my mama cooks in a Dutch oven won't end up on no cover of your *Better Homes and Housekeepin'*."

He winked at the mirror. Smiled.

"But it don't wad up in your mouth like no dishrag, neither."

Monday is his favorite day of the week. He likes the feeling that the world, though he has almost no interaction with it anymore, is bringing itself back up to speed. Getting things done. Offices and stores are open. The stock exchange—as far removed from his hilltop as it is from his curiosity—is frantic with activity after the opening bell. The energy of enterprise is running at full throttle on a Monday, he likes to think.

One of the small results of all that commotion is the arrival of letters and statements in his small box at the post office in town. Number 62. Combination 7–8–6.

Today is a Monday. But he hasn't made his usual trip. Whatever mail is in number 62 will just have to stay there until somebody remembers to take it out.

This morning he took his usual walk after breakfast and then showered and put on a pair of khakis and his favorite plaid wool shirt and L. L. Bean boots. He puttered around the house for long enough to convince himself that nothing else needed doing. Called his daughter in California just to say hello. She wished him a happy Thanksgiving, just in case, she said, they didn't talk again in the next few weeks. At the end he told her he loved her and wondered if he usually said that at the conclusion of their not-too-frequent conversations. Then he stood for a long moment with the phone still in his hand and decided not to make another call.

Now he puts a couple of cheese sandwiches and an apple that he's cut into wedges into a plastic grocery sack. He takes three small bottles of water out of the refrigerator and puts them in with the rest, then looks out the window over the sink.

The northern sky is still bright blue. Cloudless.

He hasn't listened to reports on the radio or turned on the Weather Channel all morning and doesn't intend to. What he doesn't want is the pinpoint accuracy of modern meteorology, the exact time of arrival.

What he wants is the vigil.

In a few minutes he'll step down off his front porch and walk under the old cottonwood and up the hill, past the blackened patch where the fire was, and locate the best vantage point. The most comfortable fence post to lean against.

Then he'll wait.

He checks the items in the sack and ties the top in a knot.

He might be wrong about this, of course. It's been on his mind. God knows he's been wrong about enough in nearly three-quarters of a century. He knows that the middle part, all of four decades, was wrong. Or most of it. And forty years is proof sufficient that somebody can get things very wrong indeed.

So maybe he's wrong about this. He might collect his mail tomorrow morning and then go eat lunch with Eugene like on any normal day. Then he might drive back here and build a fire in the fireplace and finish reading the novel that still lies open beside his bed.

He grins as if this is the silliest of ideas, then lifts up the sack and walks into the next room. He looks at where the old radio used to be, then at specific places where specific people used to sit.

He looks at the cold, clean fireplace where an entire forest of split oak and pecan wood was burned.

On the porch he hesitates only long enough to see if anyone is watching him from the yard.

When he's sure he's alone—that he hasn't generated enough interest for an appearance—he steps down off the porch and moves toward the gate.

three

the women under the trees

i

"Be a good afternoon for a round," Aimee's friend said. He took a long drink of iced tea; the sprig of fresh mint fell into his bread plate. One of the white-coated waiters was beside him at once, refilling the crystal goblet.

An abundance of April sunshine rested nicely on the eighteenth green beneath the big windows. A foursome of sixtyish women putted out the last of their game before retiring to the bar. Or to the Galleria. Or to their big houses that sprawled in the shade of old trees within easy walking distance of the front gates, if they had been walking folk. Which they weren't.

"You can play, if you want to," Aimee said. She reached over and took his hand on the starched tablecloth. "Dad can fix it up."

The man nodded at that.

"I thought we were going to the village," Aimee's mother said. "I wanted to show you that bracelet at Jeep Collins."

"David doesn't have to tag along," Aimee said. "*We* can go, and he can stay here and play if he wants to." She looked across at her father. "You can stay with him, can't you?"

The women on the eighteenth were done now. They laughed and talked; one of them guffawed loud enough to be heard through the windows and swished her putter around like a sword.

"Actually, I've got to go back out to the office for a little while. But I can ask Ben to get him whatever he needs."

He looked over at the newest prospect sitting beside his daughter. "I don't guess you brought your clubs."

"Not this trip," he said, flashing a winning smile, or at least, thought the man, one that was hoping to place. "I'll go to the village, whatever that is."

The downtown skyscrapers rose up like tall sunlit mirrors over the trees. Carefully tended grass stretched along the fairways, dense and deep and green and looking as soft as the carpet under the man's shoes.

"Well," he said, motioning to the waiter, "you'll have to come back again, with your clubs. I believe it's a good course."

"You don't play?"

"Never took it up."

The young man watched him as he signed the small paper for the waiter.

"You're on the board of the River Oaks Country Club, and you don't play golf?"

"Or tennis," the man's wife said. She pushed a wide plate of very nearly untouched lobster salad away from her. "Or bridge."

She and their daughter and the prospect laughed.

"I enjoy the food," the man said. He grinned. He hoped he did. "And the steam room."

"Mom made him get on the board," Aimee said, touching a wedge of lemon to her tongue.

"I didn't make him. They *elected* him."

"Wellllll," Aimee said, rolling her eyes up a fraction of an inch, as someone might check quickly to make sure the light fixtures are still attached to the ceiling.

Her mother lifted a cold pat of butter up with a silver knife, pressed it against a roll, then laid the entire business aside.

"Already sitting on the boards of a bank and Hermann Hospital were helpful." She fluttered the long fingers of one hand in the direction of some newly arrived women. "But a dinner party or two certainly didn't hurt."

She smiled at David. A brief wisp of a smile that said this is how it's done up here. Just enough to convey the crucial lesson: We're the real goods, boy.

"Surely you don't want to spend the afternoon shopping," she told him. "Or watching us shop. Not that we wouldn't love to have you."

"Which means," the man said, "they wouldn't love to have you."

The prospect winked at Aimee, then smiled at her mother.

"Why don't you go with Will," Lauren said. "He can show you his office, and all the trucks down there. Men seem to like to look at lots of trucks."

She lifted up a small compact, flipped it open, and stretched her nose and mouth around enough to find whatever she was searching for in the mirror.

"Will's driving up to the country in the morning and won't get to see you two off at the airport. And you haven't had any time together to get to know each other. Besides, I want to get Aimee some things." She snapped the compact shut, dropped it in her purse. "You'd just be bored in the places we're going. You and Will can go off and find things to do and we can all meet at the house in plenty of time to change and go out to dinner before . . ."

She looked at her watch.

"We've got to watch the time," she said, tossing her napkin on the salad. "It's nearly two. And our tickets are for eight. There're three shops that I definitely want you to see. And then dinner." She looked at her husband.

"I was thinking Italian," she said. "How about Carrabba's?"

Will laid his folded napkin beside his plate.

"Why don't you pick up some brisket and corned beef at Alfred's, since you're going to be in the village anyway. We can have sandwiches."

She rolled her eyes. Looked at her daughter. Looked at the prospect. Looked at the man.

"Alfred's is closed, dear. I've told you that. Out of business. Besides, I think we can do better by David than *sandwiches.*"

Will drank the last of his coffee. "I like sandwiches," he said.

What he had wanted to do—what he had intended to do—was go out to the office and get a few things done and then go home early enough to have a nap before the rest of them showed up. To take his shoes off, kick the air conditioner down, and stretch out on the leather sofa in his study with the *Houston Chronicle* and the *Wall Street Journal* and get just enough read to let him drift off into a nice Friday afternoon snooze. But now he'd have this boy to entertain.

"Do you have any interest in seeing the plant?" he asked. His wife slid several little bracelets a little farther up her thin wrist. "I don't want him to feel like he has to." His daughter traced a delicate design on the back of David's hand with a perfect fingernail. "It's not very interesting."

They were all looking at him now.

"It's just a plant."

Aimee gathered up the young man's tanned hand in hers once again on the white tablecloth.

"David knows all about plants, Dad. He's getting his MBA. Remember?"

The prospect's head bobbled just a bit. Some of the sunshine from the window had nestled in his golden California hair.

"Yes," Will said. "I do remember that."

Neither of them said anything until they had driven past the gatekeeper's kiosk and then beside block after block of perfectly manicured lawns and sculpted hedges and trees, through the stucco portals of River Oaks and on to West Gray Boulevard. High above, green explosions of palm fronds floated by atop towering, slender trunks lining the sidewalks in exact geometric precision. The downtown cluster of skyscrapers shimmered like the Emerald City in front of them.

"Reminds me of home," David said, looking up through the sun roof, watching one green mass of palm foliage replace another in the cloudless, blue sky.

Will pressed a button on the dashboard of the Cherokee; talk radio became smooth jazz. He didn't know anything about treble or bass or the other options that he had been shown when he bought the Jeep. So he never fooled with those. He knew about volume, so he turned it up a notch.

"Did you grow up in Los Angeles?"

"Thousand Oaks," David said. He settled comfortably back into the plush leather. Tapped out a little tattoo on the armrest with tanned fingers. "It's close to Malibu. Have you been to Malibu?"

He smiled at that, remembering what his wife had said when David had asked, yesterday, about their beach house on Galveston. Not big enough, she had told him, running one finger around the salty rim of her margarita glass. "We can build a better one. A larger one," she had said. "But we can't very well do anything about the filthy beach down there. Or the *people* who go to it."

He told him he had never been to Malibu.

"I wouldn't mind having a place there one of these days," David said. "At Malibu. Or maybe Topanga. But I'm not tied to the west coast, you know?" He rocked his head a few times with the beat of the music. "I'm keeping all my options open right now."

Past Westheimer there were plenty of shops and a couple of sidewalk cafes, still doing a brisk late lunch trade. Sports cars and Jeeps and the occasional big Cadillac and Lincoln belonging to the generation of old money that still equated high status with big cars were parallel parked in the shade of old trees.

"I just want to live in an interesting area, I guess," David said. "A nice place. That will definitely be a big part of my decision." He nodded gravely. Heavily. As if there were enormous implications involved.

Past the museums, then part way around the circle at the fountain at the edge of Hermann Park, on to South Main and past the ornate gates of Rice and into the medical center. One gigantic hospital after another loomed up over them.

"Which one is Hermann?" David asked, then looked over his shoulder at the collection of tall, Renaissance style buildings curved around a tree-lined plaza at the corner of the park Will had pointed to.

"How'd you get on that board?"

Several words fluttered down through Will's mind, like scraps of paper tilted out of a bag. Little bits of meaninglessness that he could sprinkle at this boy who was too young and too handsome for Aimee, too drenched in California aura for Houston. *Community* came to mind. Service. Responsibility. Giving back. Snippets he had spent on reporters and used at receptions. A vintage Ella Fitzgerald standard filled up the plush interior of the Jeep; he pushed around on a little button that engaged the motor that tilted his seat down and back just a smidgen, stretched. Sighed.

"I gave them a lot of money," he finally said.

At the plant, they drove through an acre or so of new mixer trucks—Fords and GMs and Macks and Peterbuilts—the mammoth stainless steel cylinders polished and newly mounted behind the cabs. David asked him why there were so many different brands.

"The customer decides what make of truck they want," Will told him, "then we build the mixer."

"So *they're* all the same."

Will shook his head.

"Different folks want different things. Some people want a little different structure on the ladder and platform at the back. Outfits from up north need different sorts of defrost controls and bleed-off valves. Then every state has its own road laws about load weight and bridge restrictions. So our engineers have to work with the buyer and come up with the designs."

"How much does one of these things cost?"

"Somewhere around a hundred thousand. Depends on the modifications, and the truck." He waved at a worker climbing out of one of the rigs. "Big outfits have big fleets. Seventy, eighty trucks. Some have more than a hundred."

"And you're the third biggest producer in the country."

Will frowned. Lauren or Aimee had been at their work.

"Third or fourth. Depends on whose numbers you believe."

David smiled.

"Third," he said. "You hovered around fourth last year, but you're a solid third for '93."

In the office, his secretary started chattering as soon as she saw him, about letters that needed signatures, contracts that needed approval, checks that needed signing. She had handed him a batch of pink telephone message slips before she looked up to see that there was someone with him.

"Evelyn," Will said, thumbing through the slips, "this is David."

The younger man reached out and shook her hand, straightened up to let his half-buttoned light blue shirt fall open enough to reveal a glimpse of smooth, golden chest under a beaded necklace. All wasted, Will knew, on the stocky fifty-six-year-old black woman standing as resolutely before him as the meanest floor nurse in any hospital anywhere, who had been married for almost four decades to one of his shift foremen, and who had as little interest in tall, young, willowy men as she did in Hinduism.

"David needs a tour of the plant," he said, already walking into his office, "will you call somebody to come up here to get him?"

After he had made two of the phone calls, and David had been led away, he looked up to see Evelyn standing in the doorway.

"This week's new accounts are on your desk," she told him.

He nodded and kept signing the checks in front of him.

"How did Aimee meet this one?" she said, leaning against the doorframe now. "He work in that company out there with her?"

"He's an intern, I think. He's still in school, finishing his MBA."

"Lookin' for a job, I guess."

"Well," he said, looking at her over the tops of his half-frame reading glasses, "I imagine I'd be looking for a job if I was finishing up an MBA."

"Lookin' around *here,* most likely."

He kept at the check signing, laying each one carefully aside as he finished.

"He's just visiting. They're . . . friends, I guess."

"Mmm, uh," she mumbled, like the first rumbling of thunder still miles away. After another minute, he looked up at her.

"Did you want something," he asked, "or were you planning on staring at me all afternoon?"

"It bein' Friday, I don't figure you'll be here all afternoon."

He stacked the signed checks, tapped them into a neat pile, and handed them to her.

"Where's she draggin' you off to this week? Is Princess Diana in town for a fundraiser?"

He shushed her away with his hand, said he had work to do. He picked up three index cards from the desktop.

"What are these?"

"The new accounts for the week, as I told you once already."

He always called the new accounts personally, to thank them for the business. He looked at the cards. Tri-City Concrete, Incorporated. In Pennsylvania. Seven standard units on Ford chassis. Thomlison Cement Works in Memphis. Three big extension rigs, on Macks. He looked for a long time at the third card.

He was still looking at it when Evelyn came back in.

"Houston *Grand* Opera called." She made the most of the title, dragging it out, shaking her big head with each syllable. "They couldn't get an answer at your house. The trustee's box that Lauren asked for is yours for tonight."

"There's not a name on this one," he said. He handed her the third card.

"There wasn't a name on the letterhead. I can get it off the invoice."

In a few minutes, she came back in with the card and handed it to him. He glanced at the name that he had thought would be there. Laid it gently on the surface of the desk.

"Now, Jess and I will be playin' 42 with the neighbors tonight," she said. "Clickin' dominoes together and sippin' cold beer. Come on by if the fat lady starts bellowin' too loud and you want to show little Mr. California Sunshine how the rest of the world lives."

He was staring out the large window beside his desk. Evelyn watched him for a moment.

"You need somethin'?" she asked.

He thanked her, told her no.

Then she was gone. The small card lay on the brown blotter on the big desk. He looked at it for a long time. Then he swiveled around in his chair and looked out the window, at row upon row of mixer trucks in the lot outside, their newly fabricated, polished cylinders sparkling in the afternoon sun like so many gigantic eggs.

David considered the abundance of plaques and framed photographs on the mahogany walls of the study in the River Oaks house. He stopped at a picture of Will and Lauren standing with another couple.

"The president," he said.

"That was my sixtieth birthday," Will said, pouring scotch into two heavy glasses at the bar. "A shindig that Lauren cooked up at the *Houstonian*. The Bushes were there for something else. Not for me."

He walked over and handed one of the drinks to David. Took a sip of his own.

"Ahhh." He sloshed the ice around. Let the cold whiskey burn its way down. "That'll make Chester walk straight."

David looked at him for a long moment, registered absolutely no reaction, and turned his attention back to the display. Parchments hailing service on committees. Elaborate spillages of gratitude for various donations. A mounted gavel from the Rotary Club. Another one from somewhere else.

"This is all pretty impressive," he said. He guided one finger along a sharp ridge in the chiseled drink glass.

Will plopped heavily down at one end of the sofa that he had hoped would play a bigger part in his afternoon's agenda than it was likely to.

"All Lauren's doings," he said. "She hung them all up."

David studied a couple of the items. Tapped one lightly with a fingertip. Then he sat down in one of the two oversized leather chairs by the fireplace. Leaned up, rested his forearms on his knees, and rolled the glass between his palms.

Will watched him. And waited for whatever was coming. It might be a frontal assault, an outright request for a job. But he doubted it. This one seemed smoother than that. And it almost certainly wouldn't be an invocation for a blessing. His daughter's hand and best of intentions and all of that malarkey. As far as he could tell, that sort of thing just wasn't done anymore. Besides, Aimee had a good five or six years on this fellow, and looked, bless her, more than a little like a Plain Jane beside all that golden luster. He suspected this kid had a nice little bit of business—a bronzed and perky teenager, more than likely—going on in the undergraduate school out there at UCLA. Or USC. He couldn't remember which.

"I wonder if I can ask you a question?" David said. He scrunched his forehead tighter, squinted his eyes.

Will took another drink from his scotch. Settled back in the soft leather. Now we'll see.

"Of course," he said.

David was quiet for a moment, obviously writing the script.

"How did you do it?" He let one small sweep of one hand encompass it all. "How does somebody pull something like all of this off? I mean, the plant, the country club, River Oaks." He took a drink. Worked the next part out around an ice cube. "Aimee told me you didn't inherit."

The word itself amused him. He saw, for just an instant, the little house on its hilltop. The enormous cottonwood that loomed above it. The big pasture in the distance. He must have smiled.

"I know you probably get asked that a hell of a lot," David said. "I'm sorry if it's . . ."

Will settled deeper into the chair; he put his feet up on the coffee table. Waved the apology away. The short version, he figured, would serve well enough on an afternoon when a nap might still be salvaged.

"It's not all that compelling a story, actually."

David leaned even farther forward in his chair. He was perched at the edge now, obviously expecting to be compelled.

"After my hitch in Korea . . ."

"You got a medal," David said, as swiftly as a game show contestant at a buzzer. Will smiled; Lauren or Aimee, or both, had laid the groundwork.

"I got two," he said. "Everybody that even went got the first one. And anybody with little enough sense to avoid getting shot got the second."

Will watched him. The kid was lapping it up, as if it actually meant something.

"Anyway, I came home and went to college at the University of Houston. On the G. I. bill. Majored in engineering because I'd been in an engineering unit in the army."

"Then you invented the . . ."

"I didn't invent anything." He took a generous pull on his drink. "There's always way too much made about that. Truth is, I needed a project for my practical my senior year. I had got to the point where I didn't know if I was going to come up with anything, then I thought back to the job I'd had before I went into the army. I remembered how the chutes used to clog up on those old mixer trucks. How they'd cause a hell of a problem. So I made that my project and designed a new delivery system. Borrowed the money to build the prototype from my professor. I wouldn't even have gotten it patented if he hadn't kept after me about it." He smiled. "He was on my board 'til he died."

"And it revolutionized the industry," David said.

Will drained the last of his drink. Sat the empty glass on the side table.

"It let the mud flow a little more smoothly. It wasn't a revolution." He stretched. Yawned. "The artificial heart is a revolution. The computer. That's a revolution. This was a little bit better mousetrap. That's all."

"And you built your company around that one mechanism?"

"Oh, that was a good bit later on. It was a long time before the company."

"But, by the time you got married," he nodded toward a large portrait of the two of them, "it was up and running."

He smiled at that, too. He had often tried to image Lauren living the way he had had to then, in the early days. Neck deep in debt.

Driving all night sometimes, after full days at work, trying to sell the device to somebody. Anybody.

"Oh, sure. By then it was."

They sat quietly for another moment or two. David got to his feet.

"I guess I'll go on up and change, Lauren and Aimee should be back soon." He held his hand out. "Thanks for the story." Will reached up and shook it.

"It wouldn't make much of a movie, would it?" he said.

"I think it would," David said. He stood there for a moment. Looked at the room. At the photographs and plaques on the wall.

"It's what we all want, isn't it?"

Will looked at the wall, too.

"If it's what you want, you'll find a way to get it." He stood up, worked the feeling back into his legs that always went missing when he sat for longer than a minute or two. Poor circulation, his doctor had told him. Some arthritis, too. Not uncommon in a man his age, his doctor had said; might even be uncommon if it didn't hurt when he stood up. He smiled. He hoped he did.

"I predict you'll end up okay somewhere out there. Maybe in Malibu."

David smiled, too.

"You know," he said, sloshing what was left of his scotch around in the large glass, "I'm not committed to the west coast."

Here was just the slightest hint of desperation in the blue eyes, the tiny twitch at the corner of the handsome mouth.

Will raised his glass an inch or so. A salute. A farewell.

"Malibu for you, I think," he said. "Just like it was here, for me."

The boy thought about it. Started to say something. Then drained the last of his drink, sat the empty glass on a polished walnut table, nodded, and went out.

Will was by himself now in the dark paneled room. Late afternoon light fell at an angle through the tall windows on to the hardwood floor. He stepped over into one of the brightly lit patches.

At the border of the sloping carpet of St. Augustine lawn, in the dark shade of thick, spreading oak trees, a group of seven women, all in identical white maid's uniforms, stood in a group at the corner. He couldn't tell from that distance and in those shadows, but he suspected they were all black, or Hispanic, all of them about to be transported from one world back to another. In a few minutes, a red and white Metro city bus pulled up beside them and stopped.

He lifted his reading glasses from his pocket and put them on, then took out the card from the office and read the words again.

American Dream Concrete Company. Destin, Florida.

He read the name underneath, slipped the card back into his pocket.

The women under the trees were climbing on to the bus now. Its doors slid shut, and it moved away under the dense canopy of branches. Towards the gates of River Oaks. Towards downtown and beyond.

Towards Lyons Avenue.

"That's a tiny icebox," his mother said, sliding one fingertip along its top, inspecting it, not giving any indication of her findings, then rubbing her fingers together. "For a place this costly."

Miss Wilson, the lady who was giving them the tour, said that it was the standard size.

"It's the same size you have at home," Will said.

She looked at the refrigerator again. Opened it up. Leaned down and studied its emptiness.

"I don't think so," she finally said. "Mine's bigger."

"Of course," Miss Wilson said, producing the bright smile she had engaged several times in the fifteen minutes that they had been with her, "you probably wouldn't be doing all that much cooking anyway. Most of our residents fix maybe one meal a day for themselves and eat in the dining room the rest of the time." The smile filled up the entire lower region of Miss Wilson's face and lingered there in stages until pressed into service again.

The old woman looked at her.

"I've always done all my own cooking," she said.

Will touched the shining surface of the range top.

"You can still do it here," he said. "Or what would be wrong with eating some of your meals down there in the dining room, with some of the other . . . residents?"

He had left home early, even before daylight, and stopped at an IHOP north of the city for his breakfast. The farewells involving Aimee and David had been conducted the night before, when they had all gotten home from the opera. He looked at his watch; their flight would be almost to Los Angeles by now.

"These cabinets could be a little deeper," his mother said. She tapped a shelf solidly with her knuckle.

"Not all that sturdy," she said.

By the time he had parked under the big cottonwood tree, he had been at the wheel for almost three hours. So he'd needed to stand for a long moment by the Jeep, to let blood and feeling work their way back down into his legs and feet, before taking the first painful steps toward the porch. She'd been ready, of course, sitting at her usual end of the couch that he had bought for her several years before. Most of the furniture in the room was new, delivered by the store in Houston where he had picked the things out, all of it in exactly the same locations where the pieces that had been replaced had stood. She hadn't wanted any of it, had put up a little squall about it, but he had sent it anyway. Two pieces—the bed for her room and a new kitchen table and chairs—she had refused outright, and told the men to take them back with them. And her old chair and ottoman, Will had noticed on one of his trips up to see her, had somehow reappeared, and he knew it would be a safe bet that the new ones had found a home in one of her friend's houses, or in the parlor of the Baptist church.

She'd had her sweater on already and her purse in her lap, saying that he was later than she had expected. He'd tapped his wristwatch then and told her that he was right on time. Was, in fact, a few minutes early.

Then the subject of Aimee had come up on the way to the place, that she had telephoned earlier in the week to explain how she couldn't come up to see her this trip. Awfully busy, that Aimee, she had said, holding her purse tightly in her lap. Too busy to drive up for just one day. Finally, when several miles of hills and pastures had gone by, she had asked about Lauren, then nodded at the single, short word that he always gave.

"This is too soft," she said, after pushing down on the bed. "That thing would do damage to a person's back."

Miss Wilson straightened the covers. "You'd have your own furniture in here," she said. "This is all only to show y'all what it can look like. A showcase unit, we call it."

Will's mother looked at the bed again.

"Well, if somebody spent the night on that thing, you'd be showing them the way to a chiropractor."

Miss Wilson located the utilitarian smile again.

"All of your own nice things would be in your unit," she said.

Will's mother stepped over to the room's one window. Outside was a parking lot, a street, another parking lot, and a Brookshire Brothers' grocery store. Red and white triangles of plastic flapped in the breeze over the entrance to the store, beside a banner proclaiming double coupon day.

"All of my own nice things," she said, turning to face the woman whose smile was already winding down, "are already in a perfectly good house on a hilltop. Where I've lived for over sixty years."

At lunch, she and Will sat at a table by themselves and looked at the plates of food that had been brought to them. She had ordered lasagna. Then he had, too.

"I don't see why we had to drive all the way into Tyler," she said, gently prodding the pasta with her fork. "There's an old peoples' home in Frankston; that's closer."

Miss Wilson had already taken another family in tow and was showing them the paintings in the lobby that were on loan from a local artist's guild. Will's mother had only liked one of them, a watercolor of a field of bluebonnets, which she had said actually looked like a field of bluebonnets, unlike the other things, which didn't look like anything that she could recall ever having seen.

"Of course, the distance doesn't really matter, does it? Since I won't be living on the farm, the old peoples' home could be in Alaska, as far as that goes."

Will watched Miss Wilson lead her charges, a middle-aged woman and a much older one, from the lobby into one of the wide corridors.

"This isn't a nursing home, Mother. And you know it." He pulled his coffee cup a little closer. Turned it in its saucer. "You didn't want to look at any in Houston." He looked around the dining room. "It's nice, don't you think?"

She looked around, too. As if she hadn't taken the time to notice.

"It's nice enough, I guess. For somebody interested in such a place."

She sat perfectly upright across the table from him. Unlike other very old people that he had known, she hadn't gotten any smaller, that he could tell. His grandfather had gotten smaller toward the end, and his father hadn't lived long enough to get very old. Not even as old as he was now. Of course, he thought, it would have been difficult for his mother to get any smaller than she already was. Her tiny hands were covered with the blotches that were the badges of her longevity; she kept her hair pinned up as tight as she had for as long as he could remember.

"I can't understand why you're so set on me moving. My goodness, it's not like I'm on my last leg. I can still drive my car, still remember where it is I'm driving to, and then how to get home. Now

I realize that some eighty-three-year-olds can't do those things. But I can."

"You're eighty-four," he said, spooning dressing on to his salad. "And you haven't driven the car since your cataract surgery."

Other diners chattered at tables around them. Servers went into and out of the kitchen; elevator music droned softly through speakers mounted on the pastel walls.

"You fell that time," he said.

She gave something between a frown and a smile, then brushed the notion away with her hand. "That was just losing my footing, trying to dodge a duck in the yard." She had given the two ducks away after that, to a friend who was younger and could stay clear of them.

She lifted a layer of crusted cheese up on the lasagna, peeked beneath it, let it fall back into place.

"If you were to take a hard fall and break a hip, then you really would have to be in a nursing home. Not a place like this."

She cut into the food with the side of her fork, then pulled a piece away from the portion. Pushed at it a couple of times with the tines.

"I miss those ducks," she said, lifting up the food to get a better look at it. "They were the last living things on the place. Besides me." Will had sold all of the cattle after his father died. Years ago. And they had quit keeping chickens even before that.

She'd had cataract surgery the one time and had to read novels in large print now. She'd been brought down to Houston occasionally, so his doctor could look her over, and Will had sent her on two cruises that she hadn't particularly wanted to go on when she was in her early seventies. And had paid for her to go to the Holy Land twice with a group organized by the preacher at her church, who provided instruction and devotionals and spiritual guidance along the way and got his trip paid for and a packet bulging with tips at the end of it.

She took a bite of her food. Chewed at it slowly. Drank some water.

"I can't say as I care for this at all."

"Mine's okay," Will said, trying not to compare it to the veal parmesan he'd had at Carrabba's the night before. "Why did you order it? I've never seen you eat Italian food in my life."

She drank some more of the water. Pushed the plate away from her.

"One thing sounded about as good as another," she said.

They sat quietly while he ate, and she didn't.

"The ideal thing would be for you to come live with us," he said. "We've got way too much house for two people. I'd even have you a little private kitchen put in by your bedroom if you wanted it. You could have your own sitting room. You'd have plenty of privacy."

She was using her spoon now to poke around in a bowl of cobbler.

"I've got plenty of privacy now. Just me and the birds that come to my feeder, and every so often a raccoon or two that wander up to inspect the trash barrel." She lifted up the smallest portion of the cobbler that she could manipulate with the spoon, touched it to her lips. Chewed. "And from my front porch swing I can look out over an altogether better view than from that little cubicle down there." She pointed in its direction.

"There's a fine view from the room you'd have at our house," he said.

She took another bite.

"This isn't too bad," she said. "Not enough butter. And they've used frozen berries." She picked at it some more. Frowned. "Or canned."

Later, in the courtyard behind the main building, a fountain bubbled away in a stone-lined pool. Fat goldfish hung motionless in water that was much too blue to have occurred naturally.

"So," Will said, "I take it you don't want me to get the paperwork for us to look over?"

She opened her purse, lifted out a penny, and tossed it in the water. She leaned forward to see where it had fallen.

"I said I'd come look at it," she told him. "And I did."

She sat down on a bench at the edge of the patio. He sat beside her.

She squinted her eyes against the sunlight and was quiet for a moment.

"I just can't see living in little bits of rooms like that," she said, looking over toward the building. "Until I have to."

"Then I think we ought to think about moving you down to . . ." he started.

"You and I both know that wouldn't work." She shook her head. "I'd be as out of place down there as . . ." She looked at him. "As I don't know what."

Miss Wilson was over by the French doors that led to the lobby. Holding the papers and a pen. Smiling at them.

"I know what the ideal thing is," his mother said. "And you do, too. For me to stay right where I am." They listened to a bird singing for a minute, just recognizable over the cars speeding by on the highway. She reached over and rubbed the back of his hand with her own. Her narrow fingers scraping across his skin like a bird's claws.

"I know you worry about me," she said. "And I wish you wouldn't." She chortled out a wheezing fragment of a laugh, found a tissue in her purse, and used it to dab at the side of her mouth. "My friends check up on me. Call me on the telephone." She folded the tissue into a square, put it back in her purse. "My heavens, that telephone rings all the time. If something was to go wrong, then they'd be out there in no time to see about me."

He didn't look convinced. So she pulled herself slowly up to every inch of her almost five feet, squared her old shoulders, and played what she knew would be her trump card.

"Tell me something," she said, turning to face him. "If your grandfather had lived to be my age, do you honestly think he would have gone along with being put into a place like this? Or anywhere else?"

The fountain gurgled and spewed. The persistent bird held forth with his warbling.

"People know when they're where they're supposed to be, Will," she told him. "Where they're intended to be. And that's where I am." She took a careful step forward now. Clutched her purse tighter. "And if the day comes that I feel like I need to be somewhere else, I promise I'll pick up the telephone, and you'll know it, too."

He hoisted himself up, rocked a little to get the blood flowing, and looked over at Miss Wilson. Who, he predicted, would be deactivating the smile in not too many minutes.

"If you can *get* to the phone," he said.

She dozed now and again on the way home, and was snoring softly when they passed though the little town near the farm. Past the building that was no longer either a café or a bus station. Busses, and most other traffic, now zipped by on the interstate a couple of miles away.

When he came to a stop at an intersection in town, he looked over at her, saw a small side street, and knew immediately that it led to a cluster of little houses under big trees. Or, at least, it did once. The houses might all be gone now. The trees, too.

There had been narrow porches on the clapboard houses, and the old woman had opened a screen door to let him in. He remembered that. She must have been about the age his mother was now. Even before his father had died; about the time Aimee had been born. He recalled exactly how she had looked up at him, studying him, finally saying that he didn't look all that much like his grandfather. Seeming a little sad about it. As if she had wanted him to. Then he'd sat in her crowded living room for long enough to tell her that he lived down in Houston, when she had asked, and that he was in the concrete business, and hadn't been married for too long, when she'd wanted to know that, too. An oscillating electric fan had pushed a tepid breeze back and forth, causing a few loose stands of long white hair to float across her brown, wrinkled face at intervals. After two glasses of iced tea, he'd told her that he had enjoyed finally meeting her, that he had wanted to for a long time. That he hoped she wouldn't take it the wrong way, his coming there. He remembered that he had thanked her for her time and for the iced tea, and apologized again for stopping by unannounced, and had gone back out into the sweltering afternoon.

All of this he remembered in the time that it took to look over at his sleeping mother while stopped at an intersection and in the few seconds it took to move forward again. Then he thought, for the rest of the time it took to get out to the farmhouse, of the confused look that had overcome her when he had turned in the yard and looked up at her on the porch and said, just on the spur of the moment, that he had always been sorry that his grandfather hadn't asked her to marry him.

He thought now of the old, soft voice that had very nearly sung out the handful of words that he had often listened to over and over and over, down the years.

That he *had* asked her.

He told Lauren what he intended to do when he got back to Houston the next morning. It was Sunday, and she was home from the brunch buffet at the club. She'd been reading the Sunday papers in the den and he'd asked if Aimee and her friend had gotten back to California okay, then told her that his mother would be staying on at the farmhouse. Then he'd taken his overnight bag upstairs, leafed through yesterday's mail, checked the messages on his answering machine, come back down, sat on one of the ugly, uncomfortable chairs that she had paid a decorator a ridiculous amount to purchase for this room, and told her. All of it.

"Well," she finally said, after enough time had passed for her to absorb it, "that's quite a story." She let the pages of the paper settle around where she was sitting, her legs curled up under her like a cat's. "Quite a little secret you've been harboring for . . . what? . . . forty years? Something like that?"

The large windows behind her glistened in the sunshine. The tops of holly bushes and junipers in the bed outside were trimmed as straight below the lowest panes as the mat of a framed picture.

"I never meant for it to be a secret," he said. "I just never thought you needed to be bothered with it."

She nodded. Gave a thoughtful look.

"And now," she said, "it just suddenly occurred to you that I do need to be bothered with it, after all."

She reached over and lifted up the remote control to the television. Clicked it off. Shut down Audrey Hepburn in mid-sentence.

"I never knew how to get in touch with them before," he said.

He stood up, walked over to one of the windows, and looked out into the deep back yard and the brick wall at its edge.

"Hell, I never tried. Never looked for them. I could have located them, some way or another. The truth is, I just always left it alone."

"Is there anything else you'd like to share," she said, "now that you're in a confessional mood? Any bombings in your rebellious youth?" She managed her first smile. Though not much of one. "No, you're much too staunch a conservative for that. You couldn't have had much of a rebellious youth." She wagged one perfectly manicured finger in his direction. "I know. Were you a CIA operative?"

He put his hands in the pockets of his khakis. Frowned.

"I hadn't intended to entertain you. I told you because I've got this thing I need to do." He rubbed his eyes. He hadn't slept much at the farm. The mattress in his old bedroom was a good one—at least, he had reason to know, it was an expensive one—but he had lain awake for the longest time before finally going out to the front porch to sit and look up at a cloudless night full of stars. He'd been there 'til nearly dawn, thinking first of his grandfather, then of the old woman he'd remembered in town, and finally of the card that his secretary had given to him. Finally, he had gazed up into the pinpoints of light and thought of other things. Of how he'd read somewhere that by the time the light from many stars reached the earth the stars themselves had ceased to be. Had burned out. Or gone cold. Or crumbled in upon themselves. Or whatever dying stars do. So the stars that he was watching, he had figured out on his mother's porch in the wee hours of a spring morning, were the same ones that his grandfather had looked up at long ago. Some of them dead and gone before either of them had had use of them.

"And I need for you to know that I'm doing it. And why I'm doing it."

She uncurled her legs and dropped her feet into the deep carpet. Leaned forward.

"Then, why don't you tell me why," she said. "Enlighten me. What in the world do you think can be accomplished by your going there, after all this time? And what makes you think this is the same man?"

The card was in his wallet. With a phone number and an address.

"Or that these people would even want to see you. For that matter, why do you have to go there? We do have telephones, Will. Why drive halfway across the country when you could call and see if they even want you to come?"

She watched him at the window.

"You know how you blow things out of proportion. If it's the same people, they may not even remember you. And then there'll you'll be. In *Florida.*"

He shook his head. Went back over and sat down. The long, sleepless night was catching up with him. The long drive that he had started after coffee and toast at first light with his mother.

"I thought about all of that," he said. "They'll remember. And you were right about them not wanting me to come. I doubt very seriously that there'll be much of a reception."

Now she smiled again. A bitter smirk of a smile that she had perfected over time.

"Oh, I'll take that bet," she said. "I'll go on the record right now, that if you do this, when they find out who you are, this will end up costing us a *shit*load of money!"

Her thin neck had grown red under a gold necklace. One vein pulsed menacingly.

"And what about Aimee?" she said. "She hasn't even entered your mind, has she?"

"Aimee?" he said, trying hard to stifle a yawn. "What does . . ."

"If this hits the papers, just what is Aimee supposed to think?"

"The papers?" He had managed to avoid the yawn, but had to shake some grogginess away. "Why do you think it would be in the papers?"

"Oh, God, Will. You just never get it."

She picked up the section of the *Houston Chronicle* that she had been reading and slapped it against the couch.

"Journalists *live* for this kind of thing. If you churn this up out there with these people, it would take one phone call," she hoisted her thin index finger to show him, "from one of them to get things going."

Now she held him in a long stare. A not particularly warm one.

"I'll tell you something," she said. "You're not exactly Aimee's favorite soup of the day right now, anyway. I don't know what the hell you said to David, but she called this morning and said the distance is wide, and getting wider. And she really liked this one."

She got up and walked over to the drink cart, splashed some vodka out into a glass, lifted it up and took a sip.

"How do you think she'll feel about this little bombshell?"

During the two or three minutes that it took for her to go into the kitchen to fill the ice bucket, to return with it and then drop three cubes into her glass, he sat on the uncomfortable chair and tried again not to yawn. So the camps had been determined, he figured, and exactly as he would have predicted. Exactly as it had always been. Aimee in a private school her whole life, just as Lauren had been, when he had pressed for public. Aimee not to be bothered with an after school job in either high school or college, when he had maintained it would teach her a thing or two, and her mother had scoffed at it as foolishness. A new sports car on the day of her sixteenth birthday; another one after she wrecked the first, then another when an even niftier model caught her eye. An upscale apartment, complete with maid service, near her east coast university, then a townhouse in Los Angeles when Lauren had pulled every string within her reach to get her hired on in a company that marketed cosmetics. A membership in a spa that he suspected Aimee never went to, another one in some society that she could never quite remember the name of.

"And what am I supposed to think about it?" Lauren asked, back on the low Scandinavian couch now that curved out into the room like a tongue. "God forbid that you should consider my feelings in all of this?"

A butterfly wobbled around outside. He watched it make its circuitous journey across the width of the five windows.

"I think I did consider them," he told her. "That's why I chose to tell you about all of this; about where I'm going."

She stirred the vodka around with her finger. The ice clinked against the sides. She sighed.

"These people will eat you alive," she said. "There's no telling how horrid this will be."

Her eyes grew wider now. She turned to face him.

"Is this some cracker barrel wisdom your mother came up with up there in Hooterville?"

She grinned at the enlightenment.

He stretched his eyes wide, trying to nudge some life back into them. Remembering how his mother, who he hadn't discussed any of this with since Harry Truman had been president, had taken each step slowly up to her porch yesterday afternoon. Inching along, pulling herself along on the handrail. Careful, he had suspected, not to fall *now,* of all times, with him watching her, ready to whisk her away to some old people's hospice as dreary as something out of Dickens. He looked over at the bar cart beside his wife. At the silver bucket full of ice. At the tall bottle of Johnny Walker that beckoned.

"I'll bet she's the cause of every bit of this," Lauren said.

These *people,* she had called them. Twice. He thought back to the last time someone had attempted to instruct him regarding the behavior of these people.

Then he closed his tired eyes tight for just a second or two. Nodded.

"That's right," he finally said.

ii

The girl at the desk of the La Quinta who printed out his bill and slid his American Express card through her swiper had told him the name of the leafy foliage he had seen growing over everything all of yesterday. Over ditches and entire fields beside the interstate in southern Louisiana and Mississippi, up telephone poles and then out along the lines themselves that hung between the poles. Up the sides of barns and weaving through the framework of big billboards advertising casinos, floating and stationary.

Kudzu, the girl had told him. It had been planted to control the erosion, she'd said, and it had pretty much outdone itself.

There had been more of it all of this day, in abundance. It had grown up to the edge of the small parking lot at the diner where he had eaten a hamburger for lunch; thick vines covered with the wide leaves had wandered along the sidewalk almost up to the doors. Will had sat and looked at it from his Jeep, almost convinced, once or twice, that he could see it moving, could see the chopped leaves that some industrious soul had been after with a hoe or a machete hurriedly rebuilding themselves. Then, for one long stretch east of Mobile, Alabama, the kudzu had so completely covered creek banks and fences and trees that it looked like a heavy, thickly woven green blanket had been thrown over everything. The owners of two or three shacks had evidently given in to it and abandoned them to the carnage. It had pushed away the panes and casings of the shacks' windows and had climbed over their edges, leaving holes in the walls of greenery, like gaping, festered mouths of things that had died desperately in need of something they clearly hadn't received.

By mid-afternoon, he had left the interstate at Pensacola and driven along the gulf, one high-rise condominium or hotel after another sliding by on his left, the crowded white sand beach dotted with umbrellas and cabanas on his right.

There was none of the kudzu here, all of it pushed back or somehow killed off, he figured, by image conscious resort planners who wanted the tropical ambiance to go just so far. The water was light green at the white shoreline, then worked its way through the spectrum to dark blue at the horizon. Quite an improvement over the beach in front of his weekend house on Galveston, where the sand and the water were two only slightly different shades of brown.

Over the last couple of days, Lauren had had to concoct a rationalization, if only for herself, for his suddenly taking off from work—which he almost never did, and never on such short notice—and heading off to the Florida panhandle. And the white sand and various shades of water had served her purpose. A couple they knew from the club had often urged them to come here; had said the water was beautiful, the hotels good. The couple had even bought a condo; the husband proclaiming one night when he was well into his third martini that this stretch of beaches was where God himself goes on vacation. Lauren had nodded politely, then had said on the way home that God really ought to shop around before spending another vacation on the Gulf of Mexico. But she could at least justify Will looking things over for possible investment opportunities, or maybe a beach house.

In Destin, he had fumbled with his map, cursed the inaccuracy of it, cursed the lack of legible street signs, cursed the driver who had honked at him when he hadn't yielded, gotten directions at a service station, and finally parked in front of the American Dream Concrete Company a few minutes before five o'clock.

Two mixers manufactured by one of his rivals groaned their way through the gates while he folded his map and slipped it into the pocket on the door. Three big batching towers rose up in the yard behind the single-story office building.

The fleet was home for the day. A dozen or so trucks were parked in rows beyond a chain link fence, being hosed down by workers, all of the big mixing cylinders bright blue, the name of the company in thick red letters on white rectangles. An American flag prominent in the logo.

Inside, the place was teeming with the energy that he felt every afternoon in his own office just before closing time. Four drivers stood in a group at a desk in the center of all the activity. One of them clutching a paper in his hand, waving it in front of an enormous old woman sitting at the desk.

"They say they don't want no invoice," the driver said. "They want a work order. That's what they want."

"We don't have nothing to do with work orders," the big woman said. "Contractors write work orders. We don't have nothing to do with that."

The driver shook his head, waved the paper.

"They didn't take the concrete?" the woman asked him.

"They *took* the concrete," he told her. "But they say they want a work order."

The three other drivers erupted into a chorus of agreement and support now. The woman's voice rose above it.

"We don't even have no work orders," she said. "There's not a work order form on this place. Because we don't do work orders." She shifted her considerable weight to one side. Squinted one eye; considered the driver with the other one. "Do you know what a work order is?"

He was shrugging his shoulders as Will brushed past him.

"It's a order for work," the woman almost shouted. "We don't order no work here. Contractors order the work. We just deliver the concrete so somebody can do the work."

At another desk, a girl was talking on a telephone.

"American Dream Concrete," she said. "Can you hold?" She pushed a button. "American Dream Concrete. Can you hold?" She pushed it again.

Since no one had paid any attention to the fact that he was in the building, he didn't see any need to present himself at any of the desks. So he mumbled "excuse me" several times, slid past enough people to head down a hallway, came to a door that was open at the end, and saw the backs of three people in front of another desk.

"We move three mixers over to that job tomorrow," one of the men was saying when Will stepped through the door. "It's gotta happen."

"It can't happen," another man said, his voice showing the strain of an argument that had obviously been going on for a while. "I need those trucks all day. I told the guy that we'd run six trucks *all day*."

He stepped beside them, then past a woman holding a clipboard.

The short man sitting behind the big desk turned his attention from the two speakers and looked up at him. His hair was coarse and full and more salt than pepper; the hard features of his tanned face showed all of what Will's quick mathematics told him were his nearly seventy years. The top buttons of his starched shirt were undone, the sharp creases of the sleeves dissolving into carefully rolled cuffs at his thick, brown forearms. He wasn't any taller, but was wider in the middle, Will noticed.

The man gazed up at him for a moment or two, then took off his glasses and laid them on the cluttered desk. Removed a half-smoked cigar and laid it in a ceramic ashtray shaped like a porpoise. When he grinned, Will saw that his teeth were still sufficiently white to be used in any toothpaste commercial. He leaned back in his chair.

"Hello, Boss," the man said.

By the time they had come to the end of their walk, high cirrus clouds were strung across the pink sunset like frayed wisps of gauze. Everybody had left now; they had stood a long time watching the last two workers spray down the towers and the pavement with high pressure water hoses, Luis smoking a cigar, then letting it go out, keeping it wedged into the side of his mouth. Then the workers were gone, and they had the place to themselves.

Will sat down on the running board of the truck parked closest to the tallest of the three batching silos. Luis stood beside the structure. The name of the company and the logo were painted huge on each side at its top, visible for what Will reckoned to be at least a half mile or so in either direction across the flat landscape.

"Everything's changed," Luis said, taking a handkerchief out of his back pocket and rubbing it across his stocky neck. "No more shoveling it in, like you and me used to do. Huh, Boss?"

He made a few short, shoveling stabs with an imaginary spade. His accent was still a sputtering of dips and rises, his voice deeper now. Rougher. As if some of the gravel he had shoveled for so long had somehow worked its way into his larynx.

"All computer batching now," Will said. He looked up at the tower.

"No mistakes," Luis said. "No bad batches. Not many anyhow. Very, very few now." He moved a thick finger from side to side like a metronome set at its fastest speed. "And then it's not the computer's fault, but whoever is the . . ."

"Programmer," Will said.

Luis nodded.

"And that's not even the best thing that's happened since the old days," he went on. "Satellite tracking," he said, easing each syllable out with the respect he felt was due such a thing, pointing up through the delicate strings of clouds into the pink sky. As if the satellite hovered directly over wherever he happened to be standing.

"Now that's the best." He pivoted around on his small feet and began pointing at each of the trucks that he could see. "I know where every rig is. All the time. I know if some guy's taking his time, listening to music. Then I call him on the radio and I say 'what the hell?' No more stopping for coffee and donuts, or making a little visit to the girlfriend's house while the mud's turning in the truck and the customer's waiting with a crew ready to spread it."

"No more *Pan de Huevo* breaks," Will said.

Luis smiled. He walked over and sat down beside him on the running board. Took out a lighter, re-lit his cigar. His shirt pulled tight at his middle; each line of his dark face glowed in the muted light, and he actually looked like he was closing in on seventy. Will hadn't expected that. Either the belly or the old man.

"That little bakery's gone," he said. "The concrete yard is, too. I drive down Lyons Avenue sometimes, just to see if I can recognize anything." He nudged Luis with his arm. "The hooch shop is still there. Still looks about the same. I've thought about going in there, to see if the same guy owns it."

Luis brushed a speck of something from the starched sleeve of his shirt. Blew some smoke away from them.

"That fellow he shot that time could probably get away from him now," he said. "He'd be too damn old to chase him."

They laughed at that. Then sat for a long few minutes as the day dwindled down toward darkness. The tall silos caught the last pink glow of the sunset. Most of the cars speeding by on the highway had their lights on.

"You've done well, Luis. This is a first class operation."

"*You*," Luis said, his eyes wider. "You're the one that did well. Such a big company, and such good trucks." He lifted his hand to point, realized he didn't have anything to point at, let it drop back down.

"Now I'll have three of them. Then I'll add some more when we get bigger."

He leaned back against the mixer.

"I knew this was a place that would need lots of concrete, Boss. I studied up on it. So we moved here and I found this man who was already set up." He tapped some ashes from the cigar. "I'd done it all by then. Batching. Driving. I even worked on construction crews. So he hired me. He already had a nice outfit; he was up to almost twenty trucks. Then, two, three years later, when I tell him I want to start out on my own, with maybe a couple trucks, one tower, I expect him to get mad. I figure he'll tell me to go to hell."

He turned toward Will, tapped his arm.

"But you want to know what he did? He went to his bank with me and fixed it so I could get a loan to buy the trucks and the tower." He smiled broadly enough to fill up the place with his perfect white teeth. "He set me up to go into . . ."

"Competition," Will said.

"Competition with him." He nodded twice.

"Sounds like a good man," Will said.

"A great man," Luis said. Growling it out. He kicked at some gravel with the toe of a handsomely tooled cowboy boot.

"I paid off that note in a little over three years." He held up three stubby fingers to show him. A thick gold ring shaped like a mixer truck—two diamonds for headlights—covered half of one of them.

"You see, he knew there was enough business for both of us, and then some. What with all the new hotels—fifteen, twenty stories tall—and resorts all along the miracle strip. And all the military things at Pensacola. And he was *right*."

He pointed out into the yard.

"Now I've got thirty-three trucks. Thirty-six when yours get here."

Will nodded slowly.

"I'm impressed."

Big lights mounted on tall poles began to automatically flicker on all around them. Each one buzzed loudly at first, then fainter, then went quiet. Wide overlapping circles of light crept out over the pavement and the trucks. Insects started chirping in some bushes beyond the chain link fence.

"Boss," Luis said. "I could have bought your trucks all along, you know. Right from the start. I knew about them. I knew about *you*."

Will looked down at the ground.

"No need to explain anything about that, Luis." He stood up, stretched. Took a few painful steps out into the yard. "I was pretty amazed that you ordered these three."

Luis looked up at him from the running board. Took a long pull on the cigar. Its tip glowed red; smoke curled out into the yard.

"That's all a long time ago, Boss. Too long ago." He stood up, too. Stomped one small boot, then the other, on the pavement. Then stomped again until the hems of his Dockers were down where he wanted them to be.

"It's been long enough."

"Mary didn't seem to think so," Will said.

It had turned out that Mary was the gargantuan woman that he had heard setting the drivers straight on the difference between work orders and invoices. When Luis had brought him back out and said "You remember Will, Mary," she had locked him in the coldest gaze that he could remember ever having to contend with, and had finally muttered exactly the four icy words, that yes, she remembered him.

"Don't pay no attention to Mary," Luis said. "She just has to be—how you say—dramatic all the time. I hear her yelling out there all day long. I *beg* her to stay at home. I tell her to volunteer at the church office, if she's gotta have something to do. Shout at Father and the ladies who work down there. Go play canasta with some other old women. Anything. But she thinks the whole business will fall down without her."

The trunks and tops of palm trees at the edge of the yard were black silhouettes now against the sunset. A jet climbed up into the darkest part of the sky. Its lights blinked faintly.

"She really raised hell when she saw the paperwork for your trucks," Luis said, emitting a high-pitched sound that was a mixture of a squeal and a curse. "You should have heard her."

He shook his head.

"We never could have no children. Mary and me. So the business has been what she did. What she cared about."

He smoked. Looked up at the jet that was nearly gone now.

"And Estella's children and grandchildren, of course."

More insects had joined in the chorus from the trees. Fewer cars went by on the highway.

"I thought she'd be here," Will said. "I figured she'd be wherever you and Mary were."

It was dark now. Quiet.

"Does she have a big family?"

"Three children," Luis told him. "Seven grandchildren. It *was* eight. One got killed in a car wreck when he was in high school." He made a rapid sign of the cross. Blinked. Whispered a name too softly and quickly for Will to hear it.

"Estella's husband, Jesse, he works here with me. He's been with me from the first, you know? Him and Estella got married before we left Houston, then we all came out here; Jesse drove one truck, and

I drove the other one. Estella and Mary did the paperwork and took the calls. Set up the jobs."

Will put his hands in his pants pockets, and stared off through the well-lit yard and into the dark smudges where the cicadas were singing.

"And Estella's oldest child," he finally said. "That's . . ."

"Yes, Boss," Luis said, his raspy voice sounding tired now. The cigar had gone out again; he dug the lighter out.

"Maria."

He cupped his hand over the flame. Puffed and blew until it was going.

"Estella named her after Mary. Which was good, you know, since it turned out how we didn't have no kids of our own."

He held up what was left of the cigar, examined the glowing tip, put it back into its place in the corner of his mouth.

"She's forty now," Will said. "Maria." He listened to the word as he said it. Nodded.

"I kept up with how old she was, all along. Without even knowing if she was a boy or a girl. I knew when it was about time for elementary school. Then high school. Then I knew when he or she was twenty, thirty. Now she's forty years old."

He looked at Luis.

"I guess she's always known about me. I mean, the fact that there was a me."

Luis stepped closer.

"I asked her one time, when she was—I don't know, nineteen, twenty—if she wanted me to ask you to come here. I told her about your company. I told her we'd do it without her mother or Mary knowing anything about it, if she wanted it that way. Or I'd buy her plane ticket to Houston, I told her, if she wanted to see you."

"And she said no, of course," Will said.

Luis shrugged his shoulders.

"Are you going to tell her I'm here now?"

Luis smiled.

"I won't have to." He very nearly growled out the words. "Mary did that already this afternoon. *That* you can be sure of."

"And what about Estella?"

Luis stood quietly. Shook his head.

"Estella's gone, Boss."

He removed the cigar. Blew a line of smoke out slowly.

"Three years ago. Almost four now."

Will watched the place where the plane had been. Then watched another one make its slow way up along the same path.

He sat back down on the running board of the mixer truck. Waited for a minute while Luis continued to smoke.

"How did she die?"

"Cancer," Luis said. "A quick one, thank God. She had a strong faith, you know. It was harder on Jesse and the kids, on me and Mary, than it was on her. She made her peace with it. She even carried one of the jars down to the priest during the Easter vigil mass. When he blesses all the oils he uses during the year to baptize babies and confirm children, you know?"

He didn't know. He nodded.

"She handed Father the jar that he'd use to bless the dead. She handed him the oil he used on her in another couple of months." He shook his head. Looked sad. "Can you imagine that?"

Will nodded. Sat quietly.

"I'd like to see Maria," he said. "I'd like to talk to her."

Luis took a last, long draw on what was left of his cigar, dropped it to the pavement, and ground it out with his boot. He took an ornately tooled wallet out of his back pocket. Began digging through some photographs, then lifted one out.

"I tried to hate you for a long, long time, Boss," he said. "But I couldn't." He smiled. "Estella couldn't, neither. Hell, she never even tried. Now, Maria, and Mary. They never had to try."

He handed Will the small picture.

"That's your daughter and your grandchildren."

Will took it over to where the light was better beside one of the poles. He took out his reading glasses, put them on, and looked at the attractive middle-aged woman seated in front of a girl in her late teens. A boy of five or six was on one knee in front of the woman, her hand on his slight shoulder.

He held the photo closer and studied the woman's face. She wasn't smiling exactly, but wasn't frowning either. She had some of her mother's features—he couldn't see well enough to see if the eyelashes were the same—and none of his own that he could determine. The girl behind her looked about as happy as a girl that age could be expected to look when photographed with her family; the boy appeared to be bored with the whole business. The shot was not a very good one, probably done by their church for a directory of members.

"Where's her husband," Will asked, handing the print back to Luis.

"She divorced him," he said. He pointed to the boy. "Right after Tomas was born. He went on a pipeline job somewhere in . . . Ohio. Or Iowa." He gave a confused look that said that he didn't know the difference between the two places. Or maybe he suspected they might be the same place. "He found a girlfriend up there. We never saw him again. Thank God."

He dug some more in the wallet and lifted another photograph out. Pointed to the girl in the first one.

"Tiffany, Maria's girl, had some trouble last year. Fell in love with a boy that's not worth a damn. She married him and moved to Tampa." He snorted out an exasperated grunt. "What a mess! She'll come back, I keep telling Maria. When she figures him out."

He pushed the other photograph down on top of the first one in Will's hand.

"Here's a better picture of Tomas. Your grandson. We're having a birthday party for him tomorrow at our house. Maria lives in an apartment and don't have no room for a party." He stabbed delicately at the photo while he talked. "He'll be eight. And, I'm thinking, that's a good time for you to come over."

He looked at his watch.

"I'd ask you to stay with us, Boss. But that would just set Mary off. She'll be mad enough anyway, when you show up tomorrow. But a man should know his own child. And his grandchild. Am I right?"

But Will hadn't heard most of it. It was all he could do to keep from dropping the photograph, all he could do to remain standing given the wobbling his knees were doing. And the race his heart was running.

Here, clearly evident on the face of this small-framed boy sitting sulkily for what had to be a school portrait snapped hurriedly was the very thing that he had searched for constantly. Only to turn up now where he hadn't been looking at all. For he had looked for it in the faces of old men, not children. And now, here it was. Over a century removed from when its original had been worn by a boy this age.

Here was the exact little down-turned smile that he hadn't seen since his own grandfather had died. That had worked its way invisibly down though the generations like a marble rolling slowly down a wooden staircase, coming to rest finally on a specific step.

On this specific boy.

He turned the map Luis had drawn for him one way and then another, looking up over the tops of his reading glasses to make sure the street names on signs coordinated with the ones on the paper, winding his way slowly through a a pretty subdivision that he figured dated back to the mid-sixties. Large plants were everywhere, spilling out over lawns from curving flower beds, standing in big pots beside front doors, some of the leaves tiny, others as wide as welcome mats. He looked for kudzu. Didn't see any.

He located the handsome brick house, parked behind several other cars, and met Luis, who must have been watching for him, on a flagstone walkway.

"We're all in the back yard," he said, leading him into a tiled entryway filled with more plants in colorful pots. "Out by the pool. Tomas wanted to have a swimming party, but Mary and Maria say it's too cold to swim. Which it ain't." An unlit cigar was clasped into its usual place.

They were walking through the living room now, or a den. A big screen television took up most of one wall, a huge stack of video movies beside it. Two recliners, of the sort that Lauren would never have considered as even a possibility, were in a grouping with a comfortable looking sofa in the middle of the room, pastel colored ceramic lamps with tall shades on the end tables. A coffee table held magazines and another plant in a pot.

"Maria's not off work yet," Luis said, his voice as hoarse as it had been yesterday. "She won't work for me. Never would. Works for a dentist. She's a . . ."

"Hygienist?"

"No, no. At the desk, you know. A . . ."

"A receptionist."

"A receptionist," Luis said. "She works for the dentist I go to. She runs the place."

"Does she know I'll be here."

"She knows you're in town. Mary made sure of that. They don't know you're coming."

Will stopped walking. Touched Luis's arm.

"Maybe something like this," he said, "a party, isn't the best place to . . ."

Luis pushed the idea away with his hand.

"It's the *best* place. They won't raise hell in front of a bunch of people." He moved on toward a set of sliding glass doors. "I hope."

Outside, the late afternoon sun spilled down through full trees on to a pool and patio area at the edge of a nicely kept lawn. Multicolored balloons had been tied to strings and hovered high over the pool, and party favors sat on several paper-covered tables. An air mattress covered with more balloons and a carefully lettered sign floated in the pool. *Happy Birthday, Tomas,* the sign said.

The adults were milling around the tables or sitting in pool chairs; the children, all boys, slapped at each other and ran across the lawn. Will looked for Tomas. Couldn't pick him out from this distance. All of the adults turned toward them when Luis led him through the patio doors.

Luis introduced him to all of the adults. A few of the younger ones had to be the parents of the running, slapping boys. Some of the older ones were probably grandparents of some of the children, or neighbors, or just friends of the family. He thought he recognized some of the people he had seen in the office yesterday afternoon.

The person obviously in charge, and by far the largest in the assembly, came slowly over to him. She wore a huge tent-like thing—a kimono, he thought, or maybe a muumuu—splotched over with colorful images of leaves and flowers. Sand dollar earrings framed a smile of the most artificial variety.

"Hello, Mary," he said. "It's good to see you again." Since she hadn't offered her hand, he didn't either; he handed her the wrapped gift he had bought for Tomas. "You have a beautiful home."

She clinched her fist tighter around the handle of the spatula she was holding. Then looked at Luis.

"Go finish cooking the burgers." She pushed the spatula into his hand. Pushed him in the direction of a brick barbecue pit. Tossed the gift on a table filled with other presents. Turned back to Will.

"You," she said, "I'd enjoy a glass of wine with." She pointed toward the house. "Inside my beautiful home."

"Let him have his wine out here," Luis said, "with . . ."

But she was already halfway to the house, the big garment ballooning up around her.

In her kitchen, she poured him a glass of sangria and set it on the table in front of where she had pointed for him to sit. Then she poured herself one and sat down heavily across from him. She took a generous drink. Leaned forward, rested her ample forearms on the table.

"It's good wine, huh?"

"It looks very good," he said.

It was the sort of kitchen he wasn't used to. The countertops cluttered with bowls and knickknacks and prescription bottles. The kind of kitchen where people lived a good part of their lives. Where they actually cooked. And ate. His mother's sort of kitchen.

She lifted up the tall goblet, turning it in her big hand so that it caught the light from the window beside them.

"It's better wine than we used to all drink in the old days, huh? In better glasses than those jelly jars we had in that little place."

He smiled. She didn't.

"Better wine. Better glasses. We all did good, don't you think? You, especially. With your big company."

The children laughed and talked loudly outside the window. Some of the adults were laughing, too. The stereo was blasting out some song he had never heard. Not a Hispanic song. He guessed that it was being screamed out by one of the little waifs with bare midriffs that he had seen on television, whom apparently eight-year-old boys fancied.

Mary watched him. She didn't bear much resemblance to the girl he had known, the one who had been able to shut down the conversation in a room with a piercing laugh that he didn't expect to hear today.

"Luis," she finally said, "he can invite anybody he wants to our house. So you come here and go down—what do they say?—memory lane. With Luis." She took another sip of wine.

"Two old men talking about when they were young. That's all right. There's nothing wrong with that."

She tilted her big head to one side now. Waited a moment before going on.

"But you got to know that Maria, she don't want you here. She don't want to see you. Don't you know that?"

He tapped the wineglass once or twice with the tip of one finger.

"I do know that. Yes."

"Yes?"

"Yes."

She looked confused.

"So why did you come?"

She waited.

"You probably won't believe this," he said, "but I'll tell you why."

She loomed stoically across from him, obviously not impressed so far. He leaned forward, searched for the right words.

"Mary," he started. He tried to get more comfortable in his chair. Couldn't. Finally settled back into it. "I was taught, a long time ago, even before I knew you and Estella and Luis, that we should be held . . . accountable for our actions. For the way we live our lives. That we should hold ourselves accountable. I forgot it, you see."

He waved one hand, slowly, at five decades.

"Somehow, I forgot it. And I needed to tell Estella—way too late, I know; years too late—that I realize how I hurt her." He waited a moment, picked up the wineglass, put it gently back down again. "I needed to tell her how sorry I am about that."

He had to wait a few seconds now. Then had to wait a few more, when he tried it again.

"Now that she's gone," he managed to get out, "I need to tell her daughter—our daughter—these things."

Mary thought about it. Then she shook her head, like someone who, after listening patiently and attentively to a salesman, has determined his goods to be not worth the money. The sand dollars on her ears jingled a little.

"That's what *you* need. It's not none of my business what *you* need. I'm only worried about what Maria needs."

She almost smiled now.

"And what she don't need is for you to show up here after half of her life is over and after she's buried her mama. She don't need you, you see? She had a mother who loved her till the second she died, and a father who *did* stay. She's got Luis and me, and she's got two kids that she had to raise because she didn't do any better at picking who she started out with than her mother did."

She sat still for a moment. Then she hefted herself up, stepped over to the window, looked outside. She slid the window open.

"Don't you burn those *burgers!*" she shouted. Then she closed the window, walked slowly back, and sat back down.

"Look," she said, after another gulp of the wine, "it's all—what do they say?—ancient history. To *me.* And Maria, she never laid eyes on you anyway. Estella had a good life. Not long enough, but a good one, with people in it who loved her. A good husband. Her children and grandchildren. Us. It all worked out. So what good will it do for you to make your pretty little speech to Maria?"

She pointed to him.

"It will do you some good. That's all."

The song that had been playing outside came to an end and was replaced quickly by another one that sounded exactly like the first.

"Look," he said. "I understand the fact that you don't like me; I wouldn't blame any of you for hating my guts. And I deserve every bit of this little . . . visit to the principal's office. But now I'm going to tell you something."

He leaned up now, over the table. Like he did at board meetings when he wanted to make a point.

"I didn't come here to make speeches. I came here to tell Estella and our child, if I could find them, what I just told you. But not just that. Not only that. To help them, too. I should have done it a long time ago. We both know that. I should have done it all along."

Mary sat perfectly still, gazing at him.

"How you gonna help?"

"There must be something she needs. Luis said she works at a dentist office. That she lives in a little apartment."

After a moment, she managed a small smile. Then she nodded her big head several times, slowly. As if the solution to an especially perplexing dilemma had finally emerged.

"Take out your checkbook, Will."

She rubbed her hands together.

"Let's figure this up, and see what you owe. Of course, we could charge you interest, you realize, after all this time. But we'll overlook it."

Luis came in, still holding the spatula, the cigar still wedged in the side of his mouth.

"What's going on in here," he said. "Why don't you let Will come out and see Tomas? Let him meet some people. Eat a hamburger."

"We're figuring up his tab. We'll be out in a few minutes."

"His *tab?*" He took the cigar out. "What are you . . ."

"Let's see," Mary said, businesslike. "We should start with Estella; do you agree? For what she went through when you never showed up. And on Christmas day." She clicked her tongue against her teeth a couple of times. "That should be worth extra."

Luis was over beside her now.

"What the hell you doing?" He growled out the words. "Why are you . . ."

"But Estella's dead," Mary went on. "So you lucked out there. Sort of like a discount. So we'll just stick with Maria."

"Are you done?" Will asked.

"We need to settle on a figure, don't we?" She placed her palms down on the tabletop. Her face was darker now. The deep lines over her dark eyes sank lower, became ominous.

"So you can write a big, fat check and go on back home. Maybe you should decide how much. Go ahead. Make it out for whatever it takes for you to feel like you're all paid up."

They looked at each other across the table. Somebody outside laughed. The song finally ended. Maybe another one had started and ended; he didn't know.

"That's enough," he said.

He pushed his chair back. Stood up.

"You're absolutely right, of course. I had no right to come here." He rocked a couple of times on his toes and heels. Jump starting the circulation. "I wouldn't have had even if Estella had still been living."

He took his car keys out of his pocket. Put his wineglass on the counter by the sink.

"It was a bad idea." He looked at Luis, still holding the spatula in one hand and his cigar in the other.

"It was good seeing you again," he told him. "I'll put a rush on the delivery of those trucks."

"Full price," Mary said, not looking at him. "You make very sure those trucks are full price."

She began the slow process of hoisting herself up again.

"I'd appreciate it," he said, when she was on her feet, "if I could just get a good look at Tomas. We won't need to tell him who I am. There's no need for that now. I'd just like to see him once, up close."

"That'll be easy enough," she said. "He's out there running around like a wild Indian. And very angry at me right now because I won't let him get in the swimming pool."

He followed them back into the living room, Luis almost hidden in front of her, holding the long spatula out like a scepter in a procession.

"Will you fly back to Houston tonight?" Maria asked.

"I drove. I'll head back in the morning."

"Are you married? Got any children? Any grandchildren?" All of it as she moved toward the patio. Not looking back at him. Not caring about the answers, he knew. Just sending out words while she got him out of her house.

"One daughter," he said. "She's twenty-eight. Lives in California. She works for a . . ."

A door opened behind them. Mary and Luis turned. Then he did, too.

She was wearing bluejeans and a short-sleeved top. Her hair was cut shorter than it had been in the only photograph he had seen of her. She wasn't as dark as Mary or Luis; was even lighter than her mother had been. She had her eyes, he could tell, but not her eyelashes. Her nose was not as small. Not large, by any means, he was thinking. But not the little nose that he had thought of perhaps a million times.

She wasn't smiling, so he had no way of knowing if she had inherited her smile.

"Maria," Luis said. "This is . . ."

"I know who he is," she said.

By the end of the first day, every exit, every sign, looked like all the ones that had come before them. The interstate stretched out straight and monotonously before him like a gray ribbon pulled tight. He didn't know the name of the town where he had eaten lunch, or even what state it was in; didn't know where he would finally stop for the night. Some motel that shared a parking lot with a Denny's or a Shoney's. Or, if he was damned lucky, a place with room service. So he wouldn't have to sit with other human beings at all.

Then, a few hours of sleep, an early start, long before daylight, and all the way home.

Home.

He smiled. Maybe he laughed.

The boy, Tomas, had only come into the house the one time, still wanting to be allowed in the pool. "Everybody has their trunks," he had told them, not concerned in the least with who the old man might be who was the cause of the current commotion. "It's not even cold," he had whined, his great-great-grandfather's odd little smile not recognizable to anyone else in the room.

Except Will.

He had turned the radio off hours ago. He hadn't been able to find anything he wanted to listen to; hadn't bothered digging through the discs in the console. So the only noise had been the low humming of the air conditioner, and when he had tired of even that, he had put all the windows down and let the warm wind gust through.

He'd thought it odd, at the time, that Maria had turned her attention to her uncle first. Had wanted to know just what the hell he was thinking, bringing him here. A perfunctory point in his general direction then, not even glancing at him. Then Luis offering his only defense. Which happened to be the truth.

She'd said "bullshit!" then. Had yelled it out with the authority of someone who said it well and often.

"You knew he'd come," she'd said. "That's why you ordered the trucks."

Then Mary, at the center, all of them standing around her like planets frozen in their orbit. She'd actually been his champion for a moment, telling Maria that he only wanted to see Tomas. Just for a minute. Just to get a look at him.

"A man should be allowed to see his grandson," Luis had growled out, shaking the spatula like a pointer.

Then Maria had reached over, grabbed the boy's thin arm, and yanked him over to her.

"You want to see him," she'd said. "So *look.* Take a good last look."

And then he'd understood why she had chosen to deal with Luis first. For it had become quickly apparent, when she pushed the boy, already whining about the swimming pool again, in front of her through the patio doors, that she hadn't intended to deal with him at all.

And that had been the end of it. Five minutes. Certainly less than ten. And she was gone.

"A man should see his own daughter," Luis had said again, beside the Jeep at the curb. "A man should see his grandchildren."

He had a new mantra now, Will thought, watching the thick green foliage between the freeway and the feeder road. A new tenet for his American Dream philosophy.

"How did you know I'd come?" he'd asked him through the open window, when he was already strapped into his seat belt, had already started the engine.

Luis had lit his cigar. Shrugged his shoulders. Growled out his answer.

"What kind of man wouldn't come?"

Some large, white water birds dropped down low over the field beside him. They sailed along in the same direction that he was going for a moment, then he left them behind.

What kind of man?

He'd do that calculation later, he knew. When he wasn't tired. When he wasn't angry. When defeat and sorrow didn't cloud his thinking.

He'd sit at his desk at the plant. Or maybe on one of the leather chairs in his study at home. And he'd do a summing up not altogether unlike the one that Mary had proposed at her kitchen table.

But not today. Maybe not even very soon.

Not now, when he was so aware of them all, everyone and everything in his present and his past, moving around quietly out there in the darkness. In a slowly tightening circle. All of them advancing toward him with the tenacity and confidence of the most aggressive variety of kudzu ever planted.

The first sandwich and half of the cut-up apple had been his lunch, so he takes the rest out of the sack for supper. The last bottle of water is no longer cold, the second sandwich not as good as the first one.

He looks at his wristwatch and sees that it's been almost four hours now. Four hours of looking back down the hill at the house and the shed. Of studying the northern horizon for any sign of change in the blue sky. Of dozing off and on. And thinking.

He wishes he had brought the unfinished novel up with him so he could see how it comes out and doesn't know why he didn't. He can walk back down there and get it, of course. A trek of all of ten minutes. But he hadn't intended to go back. So he doesn't.

He used to run up and down this hill like an antelope when he was a child. The dog sometimes following, sometimes leading.

He hears a small plane before he sees it and then follows it all the way across the wide sky until it is gone.

Once, when he was nine or ten, he sat on the porch and watched a plane fly over, an uncommon sight in those days. He turned to his mother, who was shelling peas while sitting on the porch swing, and asked her how high up airplanes could go.

She thought a moment, several of the long purple hull pods still in her small hands over the bowl she was holding. Then she said she didn't know.

"As high up as birds can go?"

"Oh, higher than that," she said, "I imagine."

"As high up as heaven?" The old lady who taught his Sunday school class had taken up heaven as her theme the last few meetings.

His mother almost smiled. Made her titching sound and went back to her shelling.

"You certainly can't get to heaven in an airplane," she said.

They were quiet for a minute or two before she brushed her hands over the bowl and stood up.

"You get to heaven by living a good, Christian life," she said, "and always living the right way."

She pulled the screen door open and started into the house.

"The right way of it," he said.

She stopped. Looked at him.

"What?"

He told her that was what his grandfather always said. That everything you do ought to be the right way of it.

She frowned just a little, then tried to work it into a smile.

"I don't know that I'd pay much attention to what your grandfather has to say," she said. "About heaven."

His eyes have been closed while he remembered. Then he drifts off for a few minutes.

When he wakes up, the sky is already half-filled with the dark arrival. The air already rich with the sweet, heavy scent of approaching rain. Every tree and the surface of the grass in the pasture is perfectly still, waiting for the first fingers of strong wind to find them.

He needs to stretch after his nap.

But he sits still, also.

four

the hawk

i

Sometimes the wind worked its way down through the big pasture in sprints. Tearing through the tall grass for a minute or two, then stalling out all together, all of the green surface that had been bowing and lifting up again in wave after wave now completely still. Other times it would whip itself into a whirl, and move its spinning body through the grass like a discombobulated wanderer, or a dancer who had finally thrown off every last inhibition, snatching up leaves and stubble and blades of grass and sending them flying. First in frantic upheaval, then more slowly, then stopping in midair, finally rocking gracefully back and forth on their way back down, like the movement of a child's hands when conducting music that only he is hearing.

In autumn, the wind persistently picked away at trees, pushing some of the leaves out of oaks and sycamores and cottonwoods, leaving the stubborn ones to wait for the first good norther that would dispose of them, too.

He liked walking best then, after the broiling summer days with too much afternoon in them that had to be filled up, and before winter, with too many rainy, cold days when even sitting on the porch was sometimes an effort.

He liked blustery days the best. When a heady autumn wind pushed everything around and nudged the collar of his coat up against his neck. Even birds had trouble negotiating with the wind on those days. He'd stop and watch mockingbirds and sparrows—even crows, which he never paid much attention to at all—when the wind propelled one of them for what looked like a good half mile before it tucked its wings and darted back and got the best of it again. Even the cattle in his neighbor's field across the road had to step around a little to keep their balance in such a wind.

He carried a stick when he walked, in case he encountered dogs or snakes. It was a handsome stick, whittled from the heart of a hickory limb by his friend Eugene, who lived in town. The top, which Eugene had left a little wider than the rest—so that it would *look* like a walking stick, he'd told him—was polished bright with oil from Will's own hand. So was the middle, as he almost always carried it like a man would carry a suitcase. He'd never used the stick to kill a snake, although he had come up on several copperheads and one small rattler. He hadn't quite figured how he would go about it, suspecting that the force he would be able to muster to hit a snake would more than likely just aggravate it, and sometimes he thought it would make more sense to carry a sharp hoe. Dogs belonging to neighbors ran through his property pretty regularly, country dogs that knew nothing about fences or leashes, but none had so much as growled at him. In fact, very few stopped and considered him at all, the open countryside offering countless more interesting possibilities than an old man with a stick.

He had told himself, and his doctor, that he would walk every day. A respectable distance at a respectable pace. And he'd found that he enjoyed it so much that he walked twice on most days, long walks at the edges of the pastures and beside the trees that stood along the creek. His first trek was always after breakfast, before he bathed and shaved and went into town for his papers and his mail and, usually, lunch with Eugene at the café. Then again after supper.

It had to be very cold indeed, or raining awfully hard—a real gully washer—to keep him from his walks. He hadn't shelled out substantial cash for a top-notch slicker and a coat from L. L. Bean for nothing, he reasoned.

He had intended to do some traveling. Off and on. He and Lauren had been on lots of trips, but hardly ever to places that he cared anything about, so here was his chance, he'd told himself. He'd even toyed with the idea of buying an RV, one of the really comfortable ones, and just lighting out on the open road. *Travels with Charley*, without Charley. He'd even gone to a dealership, sat in the driver's seat, put his hands on the wheel. But something seemed wrong about the whole thing from the start. How his legs ached on long drives, maybe. How he had to ease himself out of a vehicle and prod life back into them after just an hour or so. Or maybe the idea of a seventy-year-old man with a bad heart driving something the size of a school bus was just too damned scary.

So he'd flown out to Los Angeles the one time and spent two nights at Aimee's house listening to how her new husband, Todd, was away so much because he was just getting his dot.com off the ground. Todd was busy, busy, busy Aimee had told him, her eyes rolling up like they did, but stood to make a great go of whatever service he intended to provide. Will had flown from there to Seattle. Had ridden on a boat out into Puget Sound to look at whales that didn't especially want to be looked at that day, had eaten fresh salmon prepared in a variety of ways, had watched the rain for three days before flying back to Texas. Then he'd put his luggage in the closet and hadn't traveled again, other than the increasingly infrequent short trips to Houston.

Several times, both winters he had been here, it had gotten so cold that he'd had to wrap the outside faucets with towels and duct tape. But the house was snug enough, and there weren't any animals on the place for him to tend to, and the shrubs and flower bushes in the beds were sufficiently hearty to have climbed back out into life each spring. His mother's rose bushes had died the first winter, and good riddance, he figured. They were persnickety things, she had always said, but she had had the patience to fool with them. He didn't.

On the coldest of winter nights, he'd pile an extra oak or pecan log on the fire and read, as he did most nights, whatever the weather. He'd done substantially more reading since coming back than he had ever done. He'd always glanced through the newspaper every day, and parts of the *Wall Street Journal,* and the trade magazines of the concrete industry. He'd even read a novel every now and then, if something caught his eye in the Sunday reviews. Mostly spy yarns.

But he'd never been the consistent reader that his mother had been, beside this very fireplace. On this very front porch. And nothing trivial for her, he remembered. She'd hauled some hefty tomes out here from the little library in town. Micheners. Graham Greenes. Taylor Caldwells. She'd almost lost a friend once over reading preferences. It was toward the end of her own reading days, before the second stroke, the bad one that finally landed her in the nursing home that she had successfully avoided until well into her ninetieth year. But then only for what they had both known would be a short stay. Less than a month as it turned out. The friend had said something about the Harlequin romances she enjoyed, and his mother had made a caustic remark—she had gotten awfully proficient at them by then—that Will suspected had leaned more toward insult than opinion, and had plopped them at opposite ends of the pew in the Baptist church for a few weeks.

On his trips to Houston he usually stopped at one of the big book stores and came home with a back seat full of novels. Biographies. Works of nonfiction that had looked interesting. All hardbacks, because they felt more substantial in his hands. More like books. And because, when he was through with them, he gave them to the library in town his mother had frequented.

On some pleasant nights he wouldn't read at all, but would sit for hours in the chair swing on the front porch. He had spotted some rotten wood on the old one on one of his trips north a few years before and, driven by the vision of his mother being tumbled out into the flower bed, had gone down to the hardware store and bought a new one. So it wasn't the same swing from his boyhood.

But it was hanging in the same place. This was the same porch; that darkness beyond it was the same yard. And those stars, he often thought when he stared up at them, were the same stars.

Most of them dead, he recalled.

He saw his grandfather everywhere. In every corner of the yard. Sitting at the kitchen table, or in his old place in the parlor, looking at where the big radio used to be. Under the cottonwood tree, his tall, lanky frame leaning against the fence beside where they had buried the dog called Fred. Kicking at the place with the toe of his boot.

He wasn't a ghost, of course. Will hadn't wasted any of his time believing in ghosts, and had always been a little uncomfortable around people who claimed to. There had been a period when Aimee, during her junior high days, had taken up an interest in them. Had blabbered on about them incessantly; had cited actual cases, quoting verbatim whatever boy she had been infatuated with at the time who had put the notion in her head. Healthy curiosity, Lauren had said and had bought her every book on the subject that she could find. But he had stayed clear of both of them until it all passed, the books ending up in a closet with tennis rackets and ballet slippers and countless other things that had been used once or twice. He had even been leery, as a child, of the Holy Ghost business that his Sunday school teacher had gone on about when his mother used to haul him with her to church.

The images of the old man were nothing more than the idea of him, he knew. Brought quickly to mind when his gaze rested on one place or another. Then, just as quickly, they were gone.

If there were spirits on the place, they were the ghosts of cattle, not people. Some nights, when he lay unable to sleep in his bed he could have sworn he heard them outside. Clumping slowly along by the yard fence, moving all together from one pasture to the other one, their tails slapping at flies.

Sometimes he even thought he heard one or two of them send out a long, low bawling of protest.

Perhaps at his mother's ducks, which weren't there either.

He liked Saturdays and Sundays least of all.

Not that his daily schedule differed greatly on weekends. But he liked knowing that the rest of the world down there, below his hilltop, was at its business. That stores and banks and schools were open. That traffic was congested on Loop 610 in Houston. Even the weekend format of Tyler's National Public Radio station that he listened to every morning—classical music instead of the news and commentary program he liked on weekdays—was enough to put him a little askew. A little off his feed, as Eugene would say.

There was nothing quite so lonely, he had determined, as a Sunday afternoon.

It had been one of his concerns, of course, when he had come back. Getting lonely. But he had lunch with Eugene nearly every day on weekdays, and he usually fell into conversations with people at the post office or the grocery store. But on Sunday afternoons even someone waving from their car or pickup on the highway was something of a blessing. Nobody ever stopped by to say hello, of course. Except Eugene. Who never came on Sundays.

He was a puzzlement, he realized, to the people here. What sort of odd duck, they surely wondered, would leave what he had been, and where he had lived, to come back here. Not only to the town, but to the same little house where he had started out. How he must miss all of it, he imagined them saying to themselves. And to each other.

And he did miss things. They would have been right about that. Almost fifty years in a city would make a man miss parts of it. He got hungry for the bacon, lettuce, and tomato sandwiches that only the 59 Diner could make properly. He missed the daily routine of going to work. And the omelets at the River Oaks Country Club, where the chef knew the precise mixture of ingredients that he favored. And he wished for the sauna there whenever he woke up with congestion that needed to be sweated out.

But the occasional loneliness and missing things were usually relieved by something as simple as watching birds float high up over everything, and sometimes deer feeding at the edges of pastures. By watching the wind wander through the grass. Usually, such things were companionship enough.

The little tugging in his chest had become something of a companion also. It hadn't started out as much, just a wispy, hollow business. Now it came oftener. Louder.

Before he came here, his doctor had poked and listened. Ran an EKG. Then he'd been sent up through the hierarchy of Houston's medical royalty with a rapidity available only to wealthy donors. Of cash, not organs. Until finally he had sat one afternoon across a wide desk from Michael Debakey himself. Who used a ridiculously long word that was not at all helpful, then mumbled that it wasn't a malformation, but a disease. Probably passed down to him, he'd said, by somebody that might not even have known that they had it.

Will had looked at the film clamped on a lighted viewer on the desk, but he hadn't seen his own heart there. Surprisingly enough, he'd glimpsed his father, between the shed and the back porch. The side of his face flat against the hard ground, his big hand still curved around the edge of the box of Mason jars he had been bringing to Will's mother.

"We can treat it," Doctor Debakey had told him. "But there's not a lot of surgery we can do for something like this."

Which had been fine with Will, who hadn't been interested in a lot of surgery.

Nor even a little.

"If Wanda could make meat loaf like this," Eugene said, dragging what was left of a roll through what was left on his plate, "I'd eat at home." He lifted up the bread. Took a bite. Chewed slowly. "And avoid all the abuse I let myself in for down here."

Meg, the waitress, topped off the plastic tumbler in front of him with iced tea.

"You don't come in here because of Billie's cooking," she said. "You come to talk."

She picked up her tip from another table. Stuffed the dollar bill in her bluejeans pocket.

"Or to do *all* the talking, I ought to say. Since nobody else gets to do much of it. Mr. Will here don't hardly ever get to say a word."

Eugene took off the pair of heavy, horn-rimmed glasses that housed prescription lenses as dark as sunshades, wiped them with a napkin, then put them back on.

"He doesn't need to do any of the talking," he said. "He just needs to listen. Maybe he'll learn something."

He leaned back now, stretched his shoulders. What sparse gray hair he had was all at the back of his narrow head, with just a few wayward strands left for over his ears.

"I was always smarter than him, you see. Even back in grade school."

Meg was at the counter now, dropping change into a man's hand.

"Is that right?" she said. "I guess that about explains why he went down to Houston and ended up owning that big factory. And you ended up climbing poles for the telephone company."

Eugene finished his food, dabbed at his mouth with the napkin, tossed it beside the plate.

"He didn't go down there intending to own a factory," he said. "He went down there intending to get just enough of a job to get along, if I recall. Which I do."

Billie, the cook, ground out a short series of hacking coughs on the other side of the serving window. The bell over the door jingled when the customer who had paid his bill left.

"It took him a long time to build that company. When, if he had just asked me go with him, to advise him, we'd have had us a lucrative company up and running inside of the first month."

Meg nodded. Took somebody else's money.

"Anyway," Eugene said, turning back to Will, "what I was trying to say, before somebody kept interrupting me, was that Rush believes that kids today will end up remembering exactly where they were when they heard about 9/11. The same way we remember where we were when we heard about Pearl Harbor."

Will paid the same careful attention to him that he always did, whatever he happened to be talking about. They'd known each other all their lives, but each had had much closer friends when they were young. Then hadn't seen each other at all during all those other years. So Will had been surprised, not even a month after his return to his hilltop, to realize that he had fallen into very nearly a daily routine with this retired utility worker he had swapped a couple of unimpressive punches with when they had been teenagers.

"*Do* you remember exactly where you were when you heard about Pearl Harbor?" Will asked him.

"Hell," Meg said, delivering another plate of meat loaf, new potatoes, and English peas to another table. "I doubt he remembers where he was when he heard about 9/11."

The people at the other tables laughed at that. Will did too. Even Billie, only her baseball cap visible through the serving window behind the counter, managed to work a little laughter into the coughs.

"It might interest you to know," Eugene told them all, "that I was in the wood shop at the schoolhouse. I wasn't but nine, but, if I do say so myself, I was already mighty handy with wood. My daddy had opened up the shop for me on a Sunday afternoon to work on a bird feeder I was making Mama for Christmas. Daddy was over in the gymnasium, cleaning it up because the high school boys had had a game in there on Saturday night and he didn't want to have to do it on Monday. And Mr. Decker, who owned a grocery store back then, saw the door open and ran in there and told him he had heard it on the radio."

He leaned back in his chair. Looked around.

"Now how's that for a memory?"

He was still handy with wood. He'd made a small shelf and a paper towel dispenser for Meg and Billie, and for Will he had crafted, in addition to the walking stick, two birdhouses and a bulky letter holder that sat on top of his dresser and would have thrown Lauren into a fit of laughter. Will, who was handy at nothing, had reciprocated with books about woodworking from a Houston bookstore.

One of the other men told where he had been on that day in 1941. Then a woman at another table. Will stirred creamer into the coffee that Meg had just poured for him, saw in the swirling tan liquid his father turning the knob on the radio in the parlor with his big hand, trying to get a clearer signal. His mother, upset by the news that spilled hurriedly out of the wooden box, looking from one to another of them, but mostly at his father. Her eyes wider than usual. Something in her knowing already, he had always suspected, that whatever the crackling noise meant would pull him away from them.

One more of the diners recounted where he had been. Another said he remembered where he was, but just never had been able to recall why he had been there. Everybody listened, then turned their attention back to their plates of food.

The clientele of the café didn't change from day to day much more than the short list of items offered there, which didn't involve an actual printed menu at all, since Billie prepared one grouping of some sort of meat and two vegetables every weekday, and that was that. If somebody wanted something different for lunch, they'd either have to go home and cook it themselves, or make do with a shrink-wrapped sandwich and a bag of chips from the Zip-In Mart across the highway. Neither did she follow a prescribed pattern, where the customer would know that Thursdays always meant pot roast. Billie bought and cooked whatever struck her fancy. Chicken fried steak and mashed potatoes and pinto beans one day. Hot links and boiled cabbage and baked beans another. The loyal patrons of the place simply ate what was put before them and had no way of predicting what it might be.

Nobody in town knew if it was Meg or Billie who owned the place, any more than anyone knew for certain if they were lesbians. They'd come here from Texarkana eight years before, both of them hovering around fifty, on the heels of a blue norther that Eugene always said blew them in with it. In no time, one of them, or both, had bought the old Bus Stop Café, which hadn't seen a hamburger or a bus in over twenty-five years, and set up shop, serving one specific meal only from eleven 'til one, and only on weekdays. And spending most of the rest of their time drinking beer and smoking cigarettes in lawn chairs outside their trailer house, or doing those things, and perhaps some others that the town could only guess at, inside.

"Rush thinks," Eugene said, "that if we end up in a war over all of this terrorism business, then we might as well not even *try* to have a draft. Because none of these spoiled kids would go."

One of the men said that his grandson was in the army right now. That he wasn't spoiled.

"Well, now," Eugene said, turning in his chair to look at the man. "He wasn't drafted, was he, Stanton? Since we haven't had any draft since before he was even born."

Two other regulars came in beneath the jingling bell, found an empty table, and sat down. Billie passed two more plates of food through the serving window. Meg took them to the table.

The woman who had related her Pearl Harbor memory looked over at the table where Eugene and Will were sitting. She leaned forward, rested her hands on her purse.

"Did you ever meet President Bush?" she asked.

"Which one of us are you talking to, Mary Louise?" Eugene asked.

Meg leaned against the counter. Squinted.

"When in the hell would *you* ever meet President Bush?" she asked him. "Unless he happened to be at the top of a telephone pole."

Will waited for all of them to finish their laughing.

"I never met this one," he told the woman who had asked. "He's not from Houston. But I met his father a couple of times. Not that he'd remember, of course. Neither time was much more than a handshake. And he shook about a hundred hands a day, I imagine."

They all nodded at that. Clinked silverware against dishes. Stirred ice and sugar around in glasses of tea. One or two of them looked over at him occasionally, no more than a glance. As they might steal a glimpse of a celebrity. Or a felon. The bell over the door jingled over arrivals and departures. Then just departures.

Eugene counted out coins that had accumulated in the ashtray of his pickup to pay for his meal.

"I think I've located you a boy to come out there to cut down those trees and haul them off." He told Will. He paid close attention to his counting, wanting to get rid of as many pennies as he could.

"He graduates high school this year and is trying to make him a little money here and there. Shit."

He started over counting out the pennies.

"He's hauled hay out there on your place, for the fella that you let cut and bale. Said he thinks he knows which trees you're talking about."

A couple of small pines hampered the view of one section of the big pasture that Will remembered having when he was a kid. And he wanted it back.

"Maybe I should think twice about hiring a boy that age," Will said, laying down a dollar bill for a tip, no more or less than he had seen others leave, "when Rush Limbaugh says the spoiled youth of today are bound to be irresponsible."

Eugene pulled one stack of coins across the table into his open hand, put them in his pocket, and scooped the rest up.

"Fighting a bunch of *A-rabs* in a desert halfway around the world," he said, getting to his feet and pulling his khaki trousers up to their usual place just under the pocket of his shirt, "would call for a good bit more responsibility than hauling a few limbs down off your hill."

Later, on his way home from his walk after supper, Will stopped at the two trees. Ran his hand along their rough trunks. Kicked at a few pine cones on the ground. Then he walked far enough away to get the proper line of vision to convince himself that they had to go. He tried to determine how much he would have the boy cut up into firewood and kindling. The rest he'd have him haul off.

It was a soft October afternoon, with not more than a very few high, puffy clouds moving leisurely along from west to east. He had picked up a few bags of candy at the grocery store in town after lunch, just in case a trick-or-treater or two ranged out this far next week. But none had since he had come back, so he had bought Baby Ruths. He liked Baby Ruths.

He looked once again at the doomed trees and past them to the big pasture. What grass was left after the last cutting was still green. Still growing. Then he looked up higher to see if the regular sentinel was in residence, at the very top of the tallest sycamore on the ridge. Not today. Probably off on a last, good sweeping hunt before dark, he figured. His favorite perch, a thick limb that topped the old tree like a crown, looked naked without him.

From there, Will knew, he had an unencumbered view of most of the two pastures. Of the trees along the creek. Even, if his eyes were still sufficiently keen, of the field across the highway. Will was confident it was the same hawk he had seen constantly since he had come back. There had been stretches of time—usually not more than a day or two, several times as long as a week—when he hadn't made an appearance. But usually he saw him every day, sometimes hearing him first, his confident screeches riding along with the wind.

He'd studied him in the good binoculars he'd paid more for at an outfitter's shop in the Galleria then he would want Eugene and his other lunch companions to know about. There was something altogether different than other hawks about this old fellow's head, about the slant of it when he sat on his limb. Something about his chest, more reddish further down than other hawks. And he was bigger, of course. Older, probably.

So he had no doubt that it was the same bird that he had seen continually since his arrival. He'd heard him, in fact, when he had stepped down out of his Jeep on the first trip after his mother died, when he was still considering the move. He'd looked up and there he was, floating through a gigantic figure eight.

Sometimes, when he watched him on his perch though the heavy binoculars, the hawk was almost certainly watching him also. Just like the old black man across Lyons Avenue from the batching plant used to do.

The car slowed down on the highway, seemed to consider its next move for a moment, then turned slowly into his lane and came up to park beside his Jeep under the cottonwood. It was a sports car, he guessed, though he knew almost nothing about the makes of cars, especially low to the ground, sleek ones like this one. He stepped off the porch and watched the driver get out.

He was young, eighteen or nineteen or maybe twenty, and as slender at the waist as a girl. But his shoulders looked wide enough, built up enough, to cut down the trees. And the muscles in his legs visible in the tight bluejeans appeared substantial enough to move them off the place.

"You a hard man to find," the boy said, then fixed an expression on his handsome face that told Will he wasn't the one sent by Eugene at all.

He was at the porch now. They shook hands.

"I was at your eighth birthday party," Will told him.

The boy nodded. He wore the same type of beads that Will had seen other boys wear. That kid who flew home with Aimee that one time, he had worn them. But they had looked silly on him. They didn't on this one's dark skin.

"I remember," he said. "You gave me a Walkman. My mom made me throw it away."

He was what Will knew, from looking at the entertainment section of the paper, young girls would consider attractive. Hot, in the current lingo. He had dark hair cut a little too long, in Will's opinion, the bangs resting over even darker eyes. His T-shirt was stretched tight over the muscles in his chest and upper arms. A far cry from the skinny little whining boy who had only wanted to be let into the pool.

"How did you find this place?"

"Uncle Luis gave me a map," he said. Will had sent him directions, knowing as he put the stamp on the letter that the old man would never come.

"How is he?"

"He still runs the company. He plays golf now, but he ain't worth a damn at it." He stepped up and sat on the porch swing, without being asked. "Aunt Mary died." He leaned back against the slats. "She had a stroke; then she died. She wouldn't lose any weight."

"And your mother and sister?"

"Tiffany got a divorce. Then married another jerk and got another one. She's got three kids and works in Uncle Luis's office."

Will lowered himself into one of the chairs.

"Mom's still Mom," Tomas said, obviously not too happy about it.

They sat quietly for a long moment or two. Tomas looked at the yard, the pastures.

"What you do here?" he finally asked. "You Farmer Brown or something?"

Will looked up the hill to see if the hawk was back. He wasn't.

"I grew up here," he said. "Longer ago than you'd know anything about. When it *was* a farm. A pretty decent one."

Will realized he was staring. Seeing the little down-turned smile again, on the same porch where he had watched it so regularly as a child, was more than a little unnerving.

"Did you live here when you came to Destin that time?"

"No," Will said. "I lived somewhere else then."

The boy nodded. The perfect reincarnation of the smile nodding with him.

"You like my car?" he asked.

Will looked at it. Said it was an awfully good looking car.

Tomas nodded again.

"It's new," he said.

He gave him a ham and cheese sandwich and Fritos for supper, and some of the little Baby Ruths for dessert. Tomas drank two full glasses of milk with the sandwich and another one with the candy. So Will started a grocery list.

Tomas seemed surprised that there was a television, a large screen at that, as if he assumed that people who live out in the country can't have access to such things. Will told him that his mother had lived here until shortly before he moved back.

"She was your great-grandmother," he said, the words sounding as distant as he said them as the boy looked while receiving them.

Will told him he had had the television and a satellite dish put in for her, then had inherited them.

"I don't think she ever used it anyway," he said. "She got mad when I got rid of the old black and white with rabbit ears that only picked up the Tyler station.

Tomas sat on the couch and listened to him. He unwrapped another Baby Ruth and ate it.

"You get wrestling?" He chewed the candy. Swallowed it. "I like wrestling."

Will said he was sure he could find wrestling. The satellite in the back yard picked up hundreds more channels than he needed, since he rarely watched television at all. He'd memorized just four numbers, for CNN, the Weather Channel, a classic movie station, and one that showed reruns of *Gunsmoke* and *Bonanza*.

He should ask him how long he intended to stay, Will thought, while he watched him watch wrestling and mumble into his cell phone, so he could know how many gallons of milk and other staples to buy. But that would be rude, he realized. And he was a long way away, he knew, from asking him why he had come.

Because nobody came for no reason.

He had at least learned that.

He took his walk the next morning after breakfast and came home to find Tomas still sleeping in the smaller of the three bedrooms. The boy had been watching MTV when he had gone to bed the night before and had still been watching it when Will got up to use the bathroom and to take a pill around midnight.

By noon, he had stopped worrying about what he would give him for breakfast—he felt certain that Shredded Wheat wouldn't be to his liking even if there had been any milk left—and had started wondering what he would serve him for lunch. The daily offering at Billie and Meg's café, culinary and clientele, wouldn't be of much interest to a teenager, he knew. So, by the time Tomas finally wandered out in a pair of boxer shorts, rubbing his eyes, Will had determined that a drive to Tyler would be the best solution.

They ended up, an hour or so later, in a booth in a Pizza Hut. Where Will had eaten a plate of salad and a wedge of pizza and Tomas had wolfed down, by Will's count, seven slices, a big helping of spaghetti, and a small mountain of chocolate pudding.

"We can go over to the mall, now," Will said. "If you want to."

Tomas gurgled the last of a fountain drink out of his glass through a straw. Then he dipped the corner of a paper napkin in the ice and rubbed it against a spot of spaghetti sauce he had dropped on his T-shirt.

"You need something from a mall?" he asked.

Will watched him work at the spot. It had landed on the picture of a skeleton playing an electric guitar that was superimposed over the name of a band.

"I thought you might like to get something," Will said. "Since you didn't get to keep my present that time."

Tomas looked down at his shirt, lifted it up and blew on the spot.

"Like what?"

"I don't know," Will said. "Some CDs. Clothes. You decide. It's a gift."

Now he carefully placed the outer edges of pizza crusts that he hadn't eaten at the perimeter of his empty plate, like seven decorative timbers around a flowerbed. His brow dropped down a little over his dark eyes.

"What I need is a camera," he finally said.

Will reached into his pocket and took out his pill case. He put his glasses on and found the three that made up his midday ration.

"You want a camera? That's fine. We can get you a good one."

He took the pills and put the case away. The fluttering had grown lively the night before, as he lay in his bed, the music from the television making its way under the door. For a few minutes the rustling had caused quite a little commotion in his chest, tapping out its intentions. Maybe, Will had thought, protesting the extra person in the house. Then the sensation had subsided, and he had gone to sleep. Today, other than its usual hollow, whistling reminder once or twice on his morning walk, it had left him alone.

"I just want one of those that you send the whole thing in when you're through taking the pictures. I was going to buy one on the way here, but I forgot."

Will watched the waitress as she wiped the oilcloth covering of one of the tables. There were only two other customers in the place now, and she hadn't brought a fresh pizza out and plopped it down under the warming lights on the buffet in a while. The lunch rush was definitely over.

"We need to stop at a grocery store on our way home; we can get you one there. Be thinking of what you want to eat. Snacks and things. Anything you want."

Now Tomas was carefully stacking the pieces of crust into something like sticks in a campfire.

"You don't have to buy a lot of stuff. I prob'ly will leave tomorrow."

Will picked up the ticket the waitress had brought, leaned forward in the booth, and took out his wallet.

"While we're here, I'd like to get you something. Something that you want."

Tomas tumped the pile of crusts over with one finger.

"I just want a camera," he said.

On their way back, after buying four sacks of groceries at a supermarket and a Gameboy at the mall, Tomas sat in the passenger seat and quietly pushed at the buttons on his gift until they were well out of town.

"What happened to your company?" he asked, not looking up from the tiny screen.

"I don't own it anymore," Will said. "I sold my share to a group of investors that had wanted it for a while."

"Your share? I thought you owned all of it."

Will settled back into the leather of his seat, let one hand rest lightly on the top of the steering wheel. They were in open country now, fields full of cattle slid by. And long patches of trees.

"My wife owned part of it, and my daughter."

He looked over for some kind of reaction. Didn't get one.

"My other daughter."

The game made little muted, electronic noises as Tomas pushed at it with his thumbs. Pings and beeps.

"What happened to your wife? She die?"

Will shook his head, knowing the boy didn't see it. He thought of the initial confused look on Lauren's face among the azaleas in the back yard of the River Oaks house. Both of them standing by the koi pool. Then the *you can't be serious* stare that dissolved finally into anger. Then into lawyers. Then accountants.

"She didn't want to move up here," he said.

The game erupted into a series of pings. He'd either won or lost, Will knew. Then it went quiet until Tomas started another round.

"So you got a divorce?"

"She did. After a year or so."

A different beeping sang out over the cacophony coming from the game. Will lifted up his cell phone, listened.

"Well, that's all right," he said. "There's no hurry. He can cut them down sometime next month."

He listened again.

"No, I ate in Tyler today. I've got some company." He looked over at Tomas. "Family."

"No, I won't be there tomorrow either. That's right. I'll see you soon."

He touched a button on the phone. Put it in the console.

"You cutting something down?" Tomas said, still intent on the game.

"*I'm* not. I thought a boy from town was going to cut down a couple of trees and haul them off. But he sprained his ankle playing football. So it'll have to wait."

Tomas finished the game. Turned it off. Put it on the dashboard. He watched a huge pasture go by outside his window. A congregation of horses stood at one end of it.

"I can cut down the trees," he said, after a moment. "If they're not too big. And if you got a chainsaw. I don't want to *chop* down any trees."

Will watched that pasture play out, then some trees leaning over a tiny creek, then some hills.

"I thought you were leaving tomorrow."

He shrugged his shoulders, gave his great-great-grandfather's expression.

"I don't have to be anywhere tomorrow. I can leave the next day."

Will thought about it. Watched in his rear view mirror a little car quickly close the distance between them.

"I can get the chainsaw from my friend Eugene."

The car slid out into the other lane, swept past, slid back in front of them.

"But only if you let me pay you," Will said.

The driver of the little car found another gear, then shot off in the direction of the horizon. Tomas watched it until it was over the next hill.

"How much were you going to pay that other guy?"

Will told him.

Tomas still gazed at the empty place on the highway at the top of the hill where the car had been.

"Then that's how much you can pay me."

They sat quietly for three or four miles, watching the countryside roll by under a cloudless autumn afternoon.

"That boy was going to cut up the trees and haul most of them off in his pickup." Will said. "But I don't see why we can't just pile them up and burn them."

He leaned farther back in the comfortable seat, smiling just a little now. Pleased with the prospect of something new that needed doing.

"We'd get a ticket, or maybe even arrested, in Houston or in Destin. But people burn off brush and woodpiles all the time out in the country. I burn most of my trash in a barrel in the back yard."

He would call Eugene tonight and ask for the loan of his chainsaw. Then they could move the two Adirondack chairs from the yard up there close to the trees for them to take their breaks in. And to sit in to look after the fire. He'd make sandwiches and bring cold drinks for their lunch, or supper, depending on what time they got started.

"We can just stack the wood up and douse it all down with gasoline," he said. "And light her up."

"Like a bonfire," Tomas said.

Will smiled.

"Like a bonfire."

A boarded-up store went by now, beside an old cemetery that didn't appear interested in any new business. Then more woods and fields and hills.

"What's your daughter's name?" Tomas wanted to know.

"Aimee." He spelled it out for him. "My mother, her grandmother, always thought we misspelled it."

"She live around here?"

"California. She lives in Los Angeles."

The boy looked at him then.

"That's where I want to live."

"So did she."

After a few minutes, Tomas reached into one of the bags in the seat behind him and lifted out the disposable camera. He started reading the instructions.

"What are you going to take pictures of?" Will asked.

Tomas turned the cardboard camera this way and that. Brought it up close to look at the lens.

"You," he said.

After his walk the next morning he found Eugene sitting on his porch with a large chainsaw and a gasoline can beside him. Then he was given instructions as to how to crank it and rev it up. How to choke it, oil it, and adjust it; things Will already knew how to do. But close association with Eugene had taught him that it was best to simply listen and nod occasionally until he was done. Then he followed him up the hill to the two trees, where he surveyed them carefully from several perspectives, and showed him the exact angle that needed to be cut to make them fall where they needed to fall.

"I could go ahead and saw them down now," Eugene said, "and the boy could cut them up and haul them off."

Will touched the places that he had pointed to.

"No need to," he said. "I think my grandson is looking forward to doing it himself. He probably wants to watch them fall."

Eugene listened carefully and nodded in agreement, making no comment and asking no questions, as if his friend might have previously unmentioned grandchildren all over the place.

"How are you planning on hauling them off," he asked. "Do I need to leave my truck?"

Will told him he had decided to pile them up and burn them.

Eugene looked at the trees, then looked at the ground where they would soon be, then looked all around, focusing finally on the southeast horizon.

"That'll be all right," he finally said. "We're in for a little rain here in a bit, and then you can have you a fire on wet ground and not have a problem."

Will looked at the sky. He didn't see anything in the way of clouds more significant than a few low, unimpressive ones off in the direction Eugene had gazed at.

"The weatherman didn't say anything about rain."

Eugene was already walking down the hill toward his truck. Had already taken off his horn-rimmed glasses and wiped the dark lenses with his handkerchief.

"It won't be much of one," he'd said. "Just a little shower that more than likely made up over the gulf and is getting its exercise."

Will looked again at the far-away clouds that appeared about as unlikely to carry rain as they did snow. Then he asked Eugene how he had come to his prediction.

"I didn't spend all those years at the tops of telephone poles fiddling with myself," he told him, nearly to the yard now, heading for his truck. "I paid attention."

By the time Tomas had eaten two sandwiches and drunk as many glasses of milk, Eugene's rain shower had come and gone. Will had watched it from the porch as it moved up quickly and pushed the rain straight down, hard for a few minutes, then softer, then playing out altogether. Then Tomas had watched television while

Will had his nap and, by mid-afternoon, they carried the saw and the gas can and the two folded chairs up the hill.

Tomas felled the trees quickly enough, sending them pounding down into the wet ground in great thuds. But leveling off the thick stumps as low as Will wanted them proved a tougher task. The saw screamed out its protest and began to smoke, so after a few minutes Will told him to stop and take a rest.

The boy had worked up a sweat by then, and wiped some of it from his forehead with the back of his hand. He fell back into one of the Adirondack chairs. Looked at the two jagged pillars in front of him.

"Why can't we just pile up all the pieces I'm going to cut around those trunks and have the fire there? They're close enough together; that way I don't have to cut them off?"

Will looked at them.

"That's a good plan," he said.

"Yeah," Tomas said. "Ain't it though?" He pointed at the stump he had been battling for the last ten minutes. "I just wish one of us had had it before I wore my ass out on that mother."

While he started cutting the first of the two trees into sections, Will walked back down to the house, loaded an ice chest with sodas, covered them with ice, and rolled the chest up the hill in his wheelbarrow.

Tomas had a respectable stack of logs positioned close to the stumps by now. Will motioned for him to turn off the saw. Handed him a can and pointed to one of the chairs.

"You want to pace yourself," he said.

Tomas drank most of the soda in one tilt, then rubbed the cold can against his forehead.

"It won't take long to cut it all up, as long as that saw keeps working. Then piling it will go quick." He drank the last of the soda, tossed the empty can over by the ice chest. "It's burning it all that's going to take a long time."

Will looked at the two trees laid out across the edge of the pasture. Lifted his gaze up to the tall sycamore on the ridge. The hawk wasn't there.

"I'll help you move some of the pieces over there, then after while I'll go down to the house and make us some sandwiches for our supper."

He sat down in the other chair. Pointed to where the fire would be.

"When we light it, one or both us will need to sit with it 'til it's pretty much out." He pushed the toe of his shoe into the soft earth. "The ground's wet, but we'll still have to watch it."

Tomas leaned up in his chair. Reached over and pulled the chain saw to him. Unscrewed the gas cap and looked inside to check the level.

"If we're gonna sit up all night, we should have us some beer," he said. He screwed the cap back on. "So instead of carrying the wood, why don't you drive into town and get us some?"

Will thought he saw the hawk gliding across a far-off part of the sky. It might have been a blackbird, he knew; he had often made that mistake from that distance.

"Let's see," he said, his mind working at what it needed to, "you turned nineteen in April. Is that right? That brings you in a little short on any beer drinking."

Tomas rubbed at a spot of oil he had gotten on his bluejeans.

"Look at it this way," he finally said. "I'm sitting on my own grandfather's property. I'm not going to be driving a vehicle or operating any machinery, since I'll be all done with the sawing by then. I bet I drink a lot more beer on a regular basis than you do. And, if we're going to sit in a field all night, I'd rather do it drinking beer than soda pop." He stopped rubbing at the spot. Looked up at him. "What do you think?"

Will watched him. The hawk screamed out somewhere over the top of the big pasture.

"I think you should plan on law school," he said.

He wrote down Tomas's cell phone number and put the paper in his wallet, so he could call from town to make sure everything was okay.

When he got back, he iced down some of the beer in the cooler, made sandwiches and wrapped them in wax paper, put it all in the wheelbarrow with bags of potato chips and Doritos and a jar of salsa, and pushed the whole lot up the hill.

Tomas had sweated through his T-shirt now. Had pushed his hair back in sopping clumps over his ears. The two trees lay in sections—Will helped him move the last of the pieces over by the stumps.

Tomas lifted up the last of the logs and tossed it up on the stack. It fell into place against the stump. He pulled off his work gloves, took off his drenched shirt, bundled it up, and wiped it across his head and the back of his neck. He took a beer out of the chest, popped the top, and drained half of it.

"I'm gonna go get a shower," he said. Burped. "And change clothes." He looked over at Will. "Don't you light it 'til I get back." He pointed the can at him.

"Wouldn't dare," he said.

The hawk watched the boy walk down the hill to the house, then watched the old man sitting in one of the chairs. He had been watching their goings-on all afternoon, from wherever he happened to be in the sky, or sitting statue-like on his high perch. And now that the day was sliding down toward evening, he would go in a few minutes to make his last patrol over the two pastures and over the field across the highway and the bigger one next to it. The brief rain had no doubt turned out field mice, sending them scurrying for glistening stubble. For tender, damp blades of grass.

He would go, soon, in search of his supper. But for another few minutes he would watch the old man in the chair.

✥

They had eaten their sandwiches and chips before it had grown too dark to see the trees clearly at the far edge of the lower, smaller pasture. Tomas had brought the disposable camera back up the hill with him and had taken seven or eight pictures of Will and a couple just of the fire. By the time they had worked their way through the packages of chips and Doritos and the jar of salsa, it was night, the high stars coming out in droves now for the vigil.

The fire had roared out its arrival when Tomas lit it, sucked in all the gasoline quickly and licked long flames up into the evening, then gradually settled into a persistent gnawing away at the logs and the trunks. Pinesap oozed out and sizzled and popped, sending little sparklers up in arches, like minuscule fireworks.

Tomas and Will sat in their chairs and drank all of the beer in the cooler, then Tomas walked down to the house to get the rest of the case, and they drank some more. Will had quit worrying, an hour or so ago, about how much they were drinking. And just watched the fire and the stars. Sometimes he looked over at Tomas, the reflection of the flames dancing off his handsome features. The little down-turned, long ago smile in place most of the time.

They had talked about Tomas' high school days, where he hadn't done badly enough to flunk out, nor anywhere near well enough to distinguish himself. He'd had two steady girlfriends, neither of whom were in the picture now. His mother had wanted him to enroll in a community college and Luis—no doubt seeing the improbability of that, Will suspected—had suggested he go to work for him at the concrete plant.

He'd had falling-outs with his mom, he told him, as the beer began to make its presence known in the occasional slurring of some of his words. In the way he leaned forward in his chair to share a confidence. The way he pointed his hand at the things he was telling about little problems with the police.

The night was darker now, the fire smaller. The stores of beer in the cooler pretty much depleted. Will put on his glasses and looked at his watch. Squinted his eyes. Saw that it was after two.

Tomas was coming to the end of a lengthy chronicle about how he and a friend named Joe had planned to join the marines but hadn't. Then had planned to move to southern California and get whatever jobs they could but hadn't been able to pull together the necessary funds for such a campaign. Then had hired on as busboys at a restaurant in one of the tourist resorts in Destin.

He lifted two cans out of the cooler, tilted one toward Will, watched him shake his head, and dropped it back into the mixture of ice and water. He settled back into the chair, popped the top. Took a sip.

"I quit that damn job," he said.

He concentrated on the fire for a minute or two.

"Sumbitch who ran that place was queer, I think. Always lookin' at me, you know. He never looked at Joe like that." He laughed. "Joe ain't nothing to look at, I guess. So he stayed on. And I came here."

He stood up slowly, waited until he had his bearings, then walked unsteadily over to the place he had gone to piss several times during the night. In a few minutes, he came back and stood by the fire. Spat into it a couple of times. Pushed the end of one log deeper in.

"So," Will said, "are you going to go to work for Luis now?"

Tomas watched one glowing remnant of a log lose its balance and fall on to another one. Watched the sparks the collision sent up.

"I worked there in high school," he said. "Hosing down trucks and the towers. Sweeping up gravel." He shook his head. "Not anymore."

He drank some more beer.

"The whole damn family works for Uncle Luis," he said.

"Your mother never did," Will said. "Luis told me that himself."

Tomas was quiet. Thinking about it. Taking longer now to process things, Will knew.

"Well, I ain't neither," he said.

It was a long time before they said anything else. Will wasn't sure, but he might have dropped off for a moment or two in the interval. He was up later than he had been in years and was awfully tired. Tomas was back in his chair, already talking before he started listening.

"… to the guy, and now I got me this thing lined up," Tomas said. Still looking at the fire.

He asked him what sort of a thing.

"It's just a thing," he said, the old smile in place in the flickering light. He pointed in front of him, as if the thing was standing there. "An opportunity, you might call it."

"Tell me."

Tomas thought for a minute.

"It's like…selling things. For this guy I know in Pensacola."

"What kind of things?"

"Things."

Will nodded. He put the can that he hadn't drunk from in over an hour down on the ground.

"Drugs," he said, making it neither a question nor a statement. Just a word. Not a very loud one.

Tomas laughed. Shook his head.

"You sure are old, all right," he said. He drained the last of his beer. Reached down for one of the last ones in the chest. Popped it open.

"You prob'ly think all people my age do is drugs."

"Is it drugs?"

"It's things he gets. . .and sells to people on the base."

"Stolen things?"

"Things," Tomas said, his voice sharper now. Maybe a little angry.

"Things soldiers'll pay for. That's all."

Will managed a smile. He hoisted himself slowly up from the low chair, wobbled a little to let some feeling work its way back into his feet and legs, then walked over and kicked two logs further into the fire. He turned and looked at the boy.

"I was in the army, Tomas," he said. "In the dark ages. I know what you're talking about here. If it's *not* drugs, which I hope to hell it's not, then it's black market. Or whatever they call it now."

He stretched. Rubbed at the small of his back. Felt the alcohol at work in his system.

"And I can tell you this. It's not the best plan you ever had."

He sat back down.

"In fact, it's a godamned *asinine* plan, if you want to know the truth."

He rubbed his eyes, then the back of his neck. Stretched a little more.

"Going back to work for Luis would make a hell of a lot more sense. Not hosing down trucks, I grant you, but *driving* them. Or getting yourself into that community college, like your mother wants you to do. That'd be the best thing." He leaned back. "I'd pay for every bit of it."

He laughed at that.

"She wouldn't let you pay for *shit*."

Will turned toward him. Pointed at him.

"It wouldn't be her business. It would be *our* business."

Tomas looked at him. Lifted the can up, then dropped it down again.

"You don't know nothing about it," he said.

"I know *this*. I know that you're about to let yourself in for something that will be a hell of a lot worse than those scrapes with the law that you told me about. This won't be some little slap on the wrist when you get caught."

Tomas locked him into a cold stare now, his features hard in the firelight. He took his wallet out of his back pocket, lifted a folded piece of paper out of it. Held it up.

"This guy don't *get* caught," he said. "This guy is smooth."

Will looked at the paper. Pointed at it.

"What's that?"

Tomas turned the paper, let the light dance across it.

"I'll tell you what it is," he said, holding it up higher. "It's what's going to keep me from sweepin' gravel. And bussing tables."

He unfolded the paper. Looked at it. Stabbed at it with his finger.

"It's an address and a phone number. It's how I get to the guy in Pensacola. It's got a note on it from this other guy, telling him about me. All I got to do is show him this, and he'll take me on."

Will got up again. Took an unsteady step toward the fire. Everything spinning just a little now.

After a moment, he turned around.

"How much will you take for that?" he asked.

Tomas laughed. He carefully folded the paper, slipped it back in the wallet, put it in his pocket.

"I'm serious," Will said. "I'll give you whatever you want. All you have to do is throw it in the fire. And then forget about it."

Tomas seemed to consider it. Then he took another long pull on his beer and sat back.

"No deal," he said.

Will sat back down. He considered going down to get the bottle of Johnny Walker in his kitchen cabinet. Then thought better of it. He took a last can from the cooler and slowly drank all of it before either of them said anything.

Will looked at his watch. Shook his head.

"You were right about one thing, Tomas," he said. "I *am* old. Tonight I feel *awfully* old. And one day you'll be this old. I hope. Almost before you know it, it'll seem like. And you'll have to look back on your life, when you're old like me, and you'll have to think about just how you spent all of that time. All of those years."

He smiled and lobbed the empty can over by the fire.

"And the man that you'll be, even when you're that old and that used up, will depend on what you've been all along. On what you've done. Or *haven't* done."

He reached over and put his hand on the boy's arm.

"And the people who know you and, if you're damned lucky, love you, will have to think about all of that one day." He squeezed the arm a little tighter. "They may have to think about this damned thing you're planning on doing. This one stupid thing might end up being who you are. Don't you see?"

Tomas kept on looking at the fire. He pushed Will's hand off his arm.

Will nodded. Sighed.

"Then how about this?"

He stood up. Backed away.

"How about I just make a call to the police in Pensacola and another one to the MPs at that base? How about I give them your name, and your description, and tell them what you're up to? How about *that?*"

Tomas stood up. Wobbled. Came up close to him.

"How 'bout *this,* old man?" He tapped him lightly on his chest. "You ain't gonna do *nothin'!*"

He stumbled backwards, nearly falling. Laughed.

"You think you just about the smartest old man in the world, don't you?" He waved the can of beer around over his head, sloshing some out. "Up here on your little hill. Lookin' down at the rest of us 'cause you made a bunch of money. Thinkin' you got it all figured out."

He stepped toward him again.

"You're *bullshit!* That's what you are."

He poked his chest again. Harder.

"You think I don't know what you did to my grandma? Is that what you think? You think I don't know how you walked out on her, and then turn up—what, about a hundred years later—to make everything all good again?"

He stepped around now like a puppet whose strings had been cut. Almost losing his balance, then getting it back again.

"After everything you've done to my family, you think I'm stupid enough to believe you'd turn me in." He laughed. "Yeah, that'd make my mom just bust a gut to get to the phone to call you up and thank you, wouldn't it?"

Will moved slowly over to his chair. Let himself fall heavily down into it. He closed his eyes. Rubbed his forehead, then rubbed his chest. The boy still swayed unsteadily between him and the fire.

"Go to hell," Will finally said, almost whispering it. He leaned up and closed the ice chest. Gathered up an empty chip package, crumpled it up into a ball. "Do what you want. I don't give a damn."

Tomas smiled. Shrugged.

"That's what I figured," he said. He drank the last little bit of the beer, threw the empty can off into the night. Stood for a moment with his hands on his hips. Shook his head.

"Damn," he muttered. Spat. "Ain't nothin' worth this shit."

The fire was mostly ashes now, the things that had been logs just misshapen lumps, the two stumps nothing more than charred, smoking crags.

Will looked up at him.

"What did you say?"

Tomas rubbed the back of his hand across his eyes. Took a deep breath.

"Nothing."

After a moment, Will nodded. Maybe he smiled.

"So Luis thought it was worth the price of a new car to bribe you to come."

Tomas was looking at the fire.

"That's why you needed the camera. To prove you were here."

One of his neighbor's cows bellowed out a long lament across the highway. An owl sang out in the trees down by the creek.

Tomas turned toward him. Put his hands in the pockets of his jeans. A little dampness under his dark eyes glistened in what was left of the light from the fire.

"You're not all that great at figuring shit out," he said, his voice sad now, breaking up just a bit. Like the big radio in the parlor used to do on blustery nights.

Another owl, farther away, answered the first one.

"It wasn't Uncle Luis that bought me that car. He didn't make me the deal."

He shifted his weight from one foot to the other. Made the muscles in his neck go tight. Then let them go slack again.

"Not Uncle Luis. It was my mom."

ii

Sometimes the wind worked its way through just the tops of the trees and didn't venture down into the grass in the pastures at all. He would watch it from the porch, or from the yard, as it set the upper branches of elms and sycamores and pecans dancing, not taking any interest in anything below them.

The wind sometimes reached up high enough to bother birds that were nothing more than specks to the old man. Wind sufficient to push long lines of geese along with it, their formations stretched out so high up that they looked like the scraggly scratching of a child first learning how to put pencil to paper.

He had watched the geese for two days. Had listened to the man on the radio tell why they were about their business. Had considered calling the man who sold him firewood to bring him a cord of pecan and oak.

The boy had left the morning after the fire. He'd slept 'til almost noon, sleeping all of the beer away to nothing more than a headache, then had showered and packed his bag and said he was leaving. At his car, the old man had paid him exactly the amount agreed upon for the disposal of the trees, then told him that he had his great-great-grandfather's smile. The boy had nodded at the information, fished his singing cell phone out of his pocket, and had still been speaking into it when he drove away.

He hadn't gone to eat in town that day or the next, and had thought it must be Eugene knocking at his front door one early evening, to see where he had been. But it was a ghost that looked up at him, standing beside Batman and either a ballerina or a fairy. He couldn't tell which. He'd had to rummage through the pantry until he found three Hostess Twinkies that the boy hadn't eaten to give to them. Then they had gone down his hill, and he had the place to himself again.

His grandfather popped up here and there. Once in the bathroom while he was shaving. Another time at the kitchen sink as he washed the one dish and glass and fork and knife. He had watched him standing in the yard one early morning, staying long enough that time for him to see the bulge of chewing tobacco in his jaw before blinking him away.

And he thought of Estella more often than usual since the boy had been there and gone. He realized that he didn't know what she had looked like in any of all those years. No one in Florida had shown him a picture. And with all the photographs in the house he had been in, there were certainly many. But he hadn't thought of it then. Hadn't looked.

One night, he sat for a long time on his porch. Thinking of those eyelashes, of that little bit of a nose. And of the dark eyes that her grandson had claimed for himself.

He thought of how he and Estella would have seasoned into each other, as he had seen other old people do, given the time, given the opportunity. He thought of old men and women he had watched closely in doctors' waiting rooms, in restaurants, in parking lots. Of how they helped each other up, and looked through the stack for a particular magazine that the other would like to see, of how they touched the other's arm when there was a step. Or a curb. Or a bump.

By the fourth day since the boy had been gone, the place where their fire had been was nothing more than a black patch. Embers had glowed for a day or so, then smoke still swirled around on the place, and then it was just a scar. By spring, grass would grow over it, and it would be gone.

It was on the fifth day when he walked past where the fire had been and up to the big pasture and found what he was sure was the fence post that he remembered. The man on the radio had been talking for days about high and low pressures. About steering currents. And all those geese had gone over. Even his arthritis seemed to be more contrary, like it sometimes behaved when a change in the weather was coming. Even the wispy, hollow thing in his chest tapped out a longer message.

He eased himself slowly down against the post, found the place that still fit his back, spent a long while waiting. Watching the hawk at the top of the sycamore watch him.

He took a few catnaps. Stretched often. The final nap was long enough for the norther to have already lifted itself high up over the top of the big pasture when he woke up. The darkest of blues filled up the place behind the tall sycamore and the hawk that still watched him.

Now, he figured. Now.

It would be nice to think that Tomas would watch this norther if it made it all the way to the panhandle of Florida. It was a strong one, so it should. It would be nice to think that Tomas would feel it against his face, as the old man had felt another one at a bus station long ago. Maybe, he thought, as he stretched his back against the fencepost, Tomas would be on his way to meet the man in Pensacola.

Then maybe he would turn his car around and drive back to Destin and forget about the big plan. And maybe his mother would watch the approaching norther through the window of the dentist's office where she worked. Maybe she would step outside and let the cold wind push against her on the sidewalk.

Maybe, for no good reason that she could figure, she would hug her arms tight in her hands for just a few seconds. And maybe she would smile, without even knowing that she had done it.

He shut his eyes only long enough to savor the maybes.

In a few minutes, the first veins of lightning pushed themselves across the sky. Then the first low thunder grumbled.

The wind came slowly at first, as he remembered it would, then harder. The two or three drops of rain that stung his face were already cold, then the wind was, too.

He wasn't surprised to see the old man sitting beside him, since he had seen him all over the place in the last few days. Wasn't surprised to see the down-turned smile that he had looked at on the boy a thousand times or to see that the old man was leaning forward, as he used to like to do, resting his hard, sun-baked forearms on his knees.

But he was surprised that he was staying longer than he ever had.

He blinked once or twice, and he was still there.

He looked again at the dark sky. Felt the wind stronger now on his face. Heard rain splattering all around him. Listened to the fluttering in his chest singing louder now. More clearly. More doggedly.

He was surprised at one last thing. At feeling a little afraid, all of a sudden.

Finally, he heard a slow, easy whispering, not unlike wind in treetops. Not unlike a long forgotten tune being recalled.

"Nothing can be too bad," the whispering told him.

The next morning, all the commotion was over and done with. The front had swept completely though, wet and blustery. And now it was gone, leaving just a biting cold.

From his perch on the highest limb of the tall sycamore, the old hawk looked as far as he could see over pastures and hills. He looked down at the trees that wandered along the banks of the little creek. Then at the house and the yard and the big cottonwood beside the yard fence.

After a time, he clinched his talons tight into the limb, lunged forward, and let himself be pulled up, working his strong wings once, then twice, and sailing away from the tree out over the big pasture.

He dropped lower. Floated. He watched his own faint shadow drift across the waving grass beneath him, across the little house and the yard and the shed. He felt the cold ruffle his feathers, and lifted up now, in a wide, graceful arch across the sky.

Down on the little porch, Will took a long sip of steaming, strong coffee. He had stayed up later than usual the night before and finished the novel he had been reading. Then had lain awake in his bed and listened to the wind whistle by outside.

He yawned. Breathed in some of the cold air. Lifted up the little piece of paper that he had taken out of his billfold and read the numbers on it. In a little while, he would go inside, press the numbers into the phone and wait for an answer.

"Come back," he would say.

And that would be enough.

That would be the right way of it.

author's note

This quartet of stories grew out of a children's book I wrote several years ago called *The Boy Who Touched Winter.* It was to have been published by Corona Press and was the last book contracted by David Bowen, a wonderful man and a true gem among Texas book folk. Sadly, David passed away before the book made it into galleys, the project was dropped, and the little story settled into the bottom of a drawer in my desk.

I am grateful to Judy Alter and Jim Lee at TCU Press for seeing sufficient merit in the novel that grew out of that story that David had so looked forward to publishing.

Thanks are also due to Brij Walia, who took the time to teach me a great deal about the concrete industry. Brij is a generous and thoughtful man, whose own success story is worthy of a book of his own. Irvin Sabrsula, my physician and friend, answered many questions regarding heart disease, and Pat Soledade was, as usual, my very capable and much appreciated proofreader. Susan Petty proved to be a fine editor, and the book benefited from her meticulous attention, and Barbara Whitehead's beautiful linocuts capture the tone of the story that I hoped to convey. Finally, I'm grateful, once again, to Jacques de Spoelberch, my good warrior and dependable sounding board of an agent.